I0819973

For Nate

ROADSIDE ATTRACTION

PART TWO

TRAMP STAMP VAMP

***

Keith Blenman

Blue Donut Books

ISBN: 978-0-578-45888-5

Let's start over.

I look at my life, prior to Gus,
as a series of lessons designed
so I could learn to cope
with being blindsided.

The first time I met Gus might have been because of chest pains. The memory is erased so I know it mostly through his perspective. I see it as his past. It's only the first time I'm aware of. Maybe he'd been there for months. For all I know he was already stalking us when Wyanet dumped me earlier that year. But when I trace back through the entire chain of events- the chest pains and being awake at that late hour- that's when I know for certain he was in my life.

The pain wasn't constant. Just intermittent. Sometimes, occasionally, an hour or two after eating. Other times it seemed random. I'd wake up every night in agony, compressing my arms over my chest. Rocking back and forth. For the longest time, I avoided doing anything about it. It wasn't until my roommate, Candace, proposed a theory that I became paranoid enough to act.

"Do you think it's cancer?" she asked one night, giving a break to whatever boy she had taken to bed. Not so much as a, "Are you awake with the pain again?" or "How are you feeling?" She'd shut her bedroom door, wobbled through a pile of dirty laundry, and said, "It could be cancer. Do you feel a lump? Like, any lumps?" She had no idea how he could still hear us with the door shut. How he could smell us.

I shook my head. Unable to sleep and too uncomfortable to read or do a crossword, I'd developed a habit of playing old Nintendo games on Candace's Wii at three in the morning. It's probably not healthy, but it was either that or moping in bed, missing my ex. Or getting mad at myself for missing her. Yep, video games were healthier. While Candace was trying to have a conversation, I was trying to collect pieces of the Triforce. Exactly how this saved the world from the Ultimate Hog Monster, I wasn't entirely sure. But at the end of every dungeon there was a flashing gold triangle, protected by a beast. My duty was to slay the beasts and grow strong enough to kill the hog. Somehow, this involved triangles. "No. No lumps," I said to Candace from my gaming haze. "I really don't think cancer is supposed to hurt anyway. At least, not until the end."

"And you're sure it's not just heartburn?" she asked, draping herself onto the couch. She restacked a few dirty dishes off our coffee table and set them on the floor, creating a space to put her feet up. In some small way, I felt the mess was my fault. Between classes and homework, I was developing anxiety over the pain. Cleaning up after Candace had felt progressively less significant.

Heartburn was among the many possibilities. I'd listed my symptoms on several medical websites and they all came back with results of my impending doom. "It could be an ulcer," I said. I didn't mention that according to the Internet, it could also be AIDs, heart disease, some bacteria that eats the marrow from your bones, or yes, several varieties of cancer. Given that I'm twenty two and have never been in a third world country, the statistic likelihood of any of those is so small, I had to venture a guess that it was something else. Still, Candace had planted the seed. I killed a few monsters on the Wii and changed the subject. "So were you just coming out for a glass of water?"

Candace sighed. She quieted down to the softest whisper. "Yeah, I'm kind of hoping he falls asleep while I'm out here. Or gets bored and decides to leave." He heard every word.

"Who do you have in there?"

"Ugh. Gus."

I had no clue who Gus was. Or rather, I knew without having met Gus, he was a new toy who'd be disposed of or put away for later use. I just met Gus as a name I might occasionally hear again. A little fling because who doesn't enjoy an orgasm? Well, honestly everyone in the apartment not having one. There are some things nobody needs to listen to at any hour of the night. Candace's barnyard animal impressions of ecstacy in particular. But I'm glad she's happy. Even though, along with the noises, I have to put up with the occasional dazed, half naked man bumbling through our apartment. It's only annoying when they want to talk and play video games with me. Or when they hit on me. One guy was even surprised at my lack of interest in spite of him having just stepped out of my roommate's bedroom. "You were literally just floundering around inside the girl I split my bills with." That was a conversation for the ages.

Most of the time Candace sends them packing. For some reason, men seem to get angry at this. They call her, "Slut!" Capital S. Exclamation point. But she'll just roll her eyes with that dirty little smirk of hers. She'll shut the door and say a cool remark along the lines of, "Disposable things hating to be treated like trash." Or, "Dick is the cheapest, most replaceable economy on Earth. Whatever he calls me, we both know he's going to jack off to the memory for the rest of his life." That's her usual attitude. What's so different about tonight?

"What am I going to do, F-Bomb?" she sighed. "I don't know if I was just really hammered or what. Or why Joanie didn't stop me. He's some yokel. He's just... God you should see him. Just nasty. Actually, no. If you see him then you'll know what I've stooped to."

"Why don't you just tell him to leave?"

"I don't know. There's something off about the guy. He could still be drunk or high or whatever. I'm just going to share your bed tonight, wait until he leaves, and never talk to him again."

"You're too nice for your own good," I told her. "We both are." I lurched forward as the pain rose in my chest. I burped a couple times, which was just bizarre. Gus could smell it from Candace's room. He even had a pretty good idea of what it was.

Candace started rubbing my back as I groaned. She said, "You really should go to a doctor. I'm pretty sure you're dying. I mean, all this agony is preferred over your moping, but I can't afford the rent on my own so you should at least-" her bedroom door opened and we both looked over. An enormous, booted leg stepped out-

Or doesn't.

My memory steps in here. There's silence. There's nobody in the bedroom. There never was. When I glance to Candace, she's behind our couch, halfway to the kitchen, staring vaguely at the front door. I don't remember her getting up, but maybe I just didn't notice. "I guess the wind blew my door open?" she says.

"Did that guy leave?" I ask. "Isn't there... some guy?"

"I don't think so. Or maybe. I'm aching like it. Or maybe it was just the wind. Did you hear the wind under all that burping?"

"It sounds like your gallbladder," the doctor at the campus clinic tells me. "Of course we can't be sure until you have an ultrasound. But you probably have gallstones." He pulls out a couple of pamphlets, detailing how stones can form in the gallbladder and then get stuck, which is what causes pain.

"But I've been getting pains mostly on my left side. Don't you think it could be an ulcer? Or just stress? I'm kind of going through a break up. Well, it was a while ago. But it's still on my mind a lot."

"All the more reason to have an ultrasound. We look at everything and make sure it's all functioning okay. Sure, an ulcer is possible. Stress certainly makes one fester. But between the excess gas and the pain after meals and while you're sleeping, the gallbladder is the safe bet."

"Oh," I nod. At least Candace's theory about cancer is wrong. "Is the ultrasound expensive?"

"Two hundred and eighty dollars," the woman at the desk demands before the radiologist will see me. That's what I get for having campus insurance while having to go to an off campus doctor. It's taken two weeks to even get an appointment. I've beaten *The Legend of Zelda, Super Mario Bros. 2*, and started *Metroid.* I haven't had a good night's sleep in two months, and I think that's why it's so easy to hand over my credit card. Better broke than dead. Whatever takes the pain away. I can't study. I can't read. I barely remember the last time I sat down with my New York Times Crossword Puzzles. Even then, it was only a Tuesday puzzle and I didn't finish it. But that's okay. I've been careful with money. Even though I'm living off financial aid, I'll still have enough for rent and bills if I just cut back on food expenses. It's not a problem at all. Odds are, they'll just recommend some medicine or dietary supplement.

"No, you need surgery." The surgeon, as surgeons often do, recommends surgery. "You have sludge and some small stones. It's actually very common. I'm surprised we don't just take the silly thing out at birth."

"So it's not an overly complicated operation?"

"Not at all. Just four little incisions." He taps my gut just below the navel, then two spots on my right side, just below my ribs. Then again directly below my breastbone. It's a little too close for comfort, but he's a doctor so I don't say anything. "We fill your belly with air so we have room to operate. The scope goes in through your belly button. I make a couple of small cuts then pull the gallbladder through your chest. Simple!" He makes it sound like going to the dentist for a routine cleaning. Or changing batteries in the smoke detector. A minor inconvenience but hardly even noteworthy. Sometimes people get physicals. Sometimes they get their gallbladders removed. It's not until I pay his receptionist that it all starts to sink in.

"A hundred and ninety dollars?" Joanie's facial piercings contort a few odd folds as she lifts her eyebrows. I'm telling her about the appointment as we walk into our *Introduction to Japanese History* class.

"I felt like such a child," I say, taking my seat. "I told the lady, 'No, he didn't perform the surgery. We just talked.' She told me his standard consultation fee is two-twenty-five. I got a discount because I'm a student."

"Consultation fee?" Joanie shakes her head. "That's like having the university charge us an extra hundred bucks for the syllabus."

"Have you paid your tuition? I'm pretty sure they do."

"Shit, F-Bomb. Are you sure you even need the surgery? Maybe you should get a second opinion?"

I rifle through my bag, digging for my notebook and something to write with. The first pen I find is blue. I toss it back and dig around until I find a black one. How did I even get a blue pen? "The finder's fee from radiology and the first opinion already cost me four hundred bucks. The only second opinion I can afford is from medical websites, and they, like Candace, are convinced I have terminal cancer."

"Okay, so that's one for gallbladder and two for cancer," Joanie nods, sure of herself. She adds, "What can I say? You're fucking dying."

"Wow. Thanks Mom."

A thing about Joanie is, I met her the same day I last saw my parents. Mama and Dad were just about to abandon me forever. I didn't know at the time. I don't think they knew. They'd just moved me into the college dorms. The whole day had a palpable silence to it. Packing and unpacking. A quiet lunch. Mama looking down at her plate. Dad not so subtly keeping his eyes fixed on the nearest exit. They'd have gladly put me on a bus if it didn't look bad to their friends. Afterall, nobody knew my terrible secret. I can't remember whose idea it was for one last meal, but there was nothing familial about it. Ceremonial, perhaps, but they'd already said goodbye a year ago. This was just going through the motions. We sat in near silence, our lunch disappearing like vegetables on a toddler's plate. It wasn't until the food was almost gone that Mama said, "Millie, I want you to know, it might take time but..." she trailed off.

Dad took over. "If you ever get through whatever this is."

"That's not-" Mama started, but Dad put up a hand.

"I'm sorry," I said. If not for Gus, that apology may have become single biggest regret of my life. At least I followed it with some measure of certainty. "This is who I am."

Dad said, "Trust me. You don't know who you are yet."

Before the conversation could go further, a hulking, punked out girl with green and black hair, purple lips, and safety pins down the sleeves of her jacket said, "So, um, Lisa, your waitress, just quit and tore up the checks for all her tables. Do you just want to give me twenty bucks and we'll call it square?" She was more slender then, but still muscles on top of muscles.

Mama and Dad glared at her like they'd met the devil, but Dad handed her two tens and told her the bun for his burger wasn't toasted. She apologized and said she'll have a word with the cooks before walking off. Dad shook his head as she departed and said, "Whatever you're going to be, Emmeline, don't be that." They gave me some quick advice about keeping up with my studies before making their way out of my life, leaving me to finish a Coke in silence. At least until our waitress, Andrea, showed up with the check.

Twenty minutes later I was walking back to my dorm. I saw green and black hair under a fresh plume of smoke. I couldn't help but blush when I introduced myself...when I unknowingly started my new family.

"Please, if I was your mom, you'd have gone to college already knowing how to eat a good pussy." Joanie rolls her eyes.

I try not to squirm, but God I hope the rest of the class didn't hear that.

"Oh, there she is. The prude." she smirks. "Always so innocent. No way you could be the girl who used to dive between my legs every time the lights went out."

"Yeah. Sorry. I didn't get a chance for any of that growing up. I guess I kind of exploded when I got here."

"She admits to the barrage of sexual assault." She smiles, stretching her back. "I don't blame you, F-Bomb. It's hard to resist *all this*. I know I don't. But you really shouldn't pretend you don't have that monster inside you. Your wild side is a beautiful, wonderful thing."

"Gosh. Thanks."

Students continue to trudge in, along with our professor, Dr. Matts. "Sorry I'm late, everyone," he says. Not wasting time getting to his lecture, he fumbles through a laptop bag. "We'll begin today by touching on Jōmon, but then quickly move into the Yayoi period, where we'll be spending the next few weeks. An interesting note I always like to begin with is the somewhat recent discovery that the Jōmon-jin are actually related to Native Americans."

I roll my head back to stretch. The lecture hall door opens as Dr. Matts revs himself up. I can't help but stare, or at least linger in the moment, because the love of my life walks into the room.

"Just talk to her," Joanie says three hours later, pecking at the remnants of her sweet and sour chicken. "When she walked in the room, your head was so contorted I thought you'd actually managed to snap your neck."

"I think I'd rather just have my gallbladder ripped out." Why did I agree to Chinese after class? Everything is fried and the stabbing pain in my ribs is reminding me of it. "Wyanet's done with me. She's been done for months now."

"Yet she still sat two rows ahead of us. Shit, she never even dropped the class."

"Maybe everything else was booked?" I stare out the window. There are some streaks in the glass and my reflection is staring back. The rings under my eyes make me look like a raccoon. I'm done with this conversation; I've been done with it for six months now. At least that's what I'm telling myself. "Did you see how she split after lecture?"

Or the way her hair flowed over her shoulder when she stood. How she was wearing her favorite dangling earrings. Wyanet is every sort of lovely and wonderful, but I spent my entire teenage life pining for girls who would never, ever show interest. Lately, I'm feeling too old for this kind of moping.

If Wyanet would make a move or give some indication of wanting me back, things would be different. Eight months after breaking my heart and I'm so sick of daydreaming. Sometimes it's just nice to miss someone and enjoy the fact that I get to share a room with her twice a week. I'm going to graduate in the Spring. What's the sense in pursuing her if I'm just going to leave it all behind soon anyway? I should keep my focus on school and my future. If not that, I should at least ignore Joanie and enjoy the afternoon sun coming through a poorly cleaned Chinese restaurant window. Raccoon eyes and all.

"She's just a pussy. Like you," Joanie doesn't care I'm purposefully ignoring her. "Or she didn't want to have to climb around me to get to you. Not that it would've taken much effort, the fucking twig." She holds up one of her chopsticks and makes it dance in the middle of the table. In a Minnie Mouse voice she says, "Hey there, F-Bomb. I'm Wyanet Hoof and I'm the prettiest Chippewa in the world. Would you like to-" She cuts herself out of character and says, "Oh, wait. Too tall." She snaps the chopstick in half and continues. "Now I'm actual size Wyanet and I think you should quit worrying about your future for once and just make out with me! Don't you want to make out with me? I'm so pretty and exotic and-" she cuts herself off again to ask, "Would it help if I painted it red?"

"That's so wrong. And she's not Chippewa. She's Potawatomi." I say.

Joanie continues her chopstick dance. "Oh! Thank you for defending my honor, F-Bomb. I think chivalry is so sexy. You are my Warrior Princess. I want to put my entire twig body inside your disturbingly hairless vagina."

"Oh my god!" I bury my face in my hands. A couple at the nearest table start giggling. "Just stop!"

"You need to relax," Joanie laughs. She puts her hand over mine as the anesthesiologist injects me with something designed for just that. She says, "All those tattoos and you're scared of a fucking needle."

Candace is sitting next to her, watching the push of the plunger fill my veins with something I can't quite pronounce. "It's not a big deal," she tells me. "My grandpa had his gallbladder removed and he was fine. I mean, he died like two months later, but that was only because he had c-diff."

The nurse, Joanie, and I all glare at Candace. She takes the hint and asks the anesthesiologist if there are any cute doctors working today.

"I ain't cute enough for you?" he asks.

My head drifts into the pillow. It's eating at me that Mama doesn't know I'm having an operation today. I don't know why. We haven't spoken since Dad died. But for something like this I should've called. Or at least sent an email. Something along the lines of *Dear Mama, I'm going under the knife today. Just in case it all goes wrong and I never wake up... I don't know... Feel terrible for the rest of your life. Or don't. I don't care. Love, Millie.* I'm starting to feel fuzzy.. "Hey there," I say to nobody in particular. "What's the metabolic half-life on this stuff? Please tell me it's slow."

The anesthesiologist says, "You looked like a featherweight."

"You should see her drink," Joanie adds.

I ask, "Am I going to pass out now?"

"Not yet," The anesthesiologist says. "We save the harder stuff for the operating room. For now just relax and let the drugs do their work."

I can feel the corners of my lips tighten. Like, really tighten, and it's such an odd thing. Lips. Corners. The way a smile is a form of tightening. "Oh, thank you!"

He stares into my eyes and shines a little flashlight at my face. "Were you honest about your weight?" he asks.

"You know it."

"Okay," he says. "No big deal. Some people just have stronger reactions than others."

"Is that a bad thing?" I ask.

"Does it feel like a bad thing?"

"Nope."

"Then nope. But I'll be back in a couple of minutes to check on you."

"Oh my god. You're so kind."

Candace and Joanie are clearly amused. Candace takes a selfie with me in the background. Joanie rolls her eyes, but then takes out her phone and snaps a couple of shots. "Say *fuzzy pickles*!" she says. "You are so fucking stoned."

I'm dead sober when the bills start coming. "I thought my insurance was supposed to cover the operation," I say to some stubborn woman at a call center.

"Yes, this is true," she says. "Your plan covered the entire cost of the operation itself. However the surgeon's fees, anesthesiologist's fees, autopsy of the removed organ, and rental costs were not included."

"How are those not included?" I slump forward at my kitchen table, but wince to a sting in my navel. I had been told the stitches would dissolve, but I'm starting to wonder. Leaning too far, slouching, or even rolling over in my sleep causes stabbing pain. "If nothing else, the surgeon and drugs were required for the operation. And what rental costs? I didn't rent anything."

"Rental costs consist of the room and hospital bed."

"I was there for five hours! The first hour was in the waiting room."

"Hah," she says a laugh. "I assure you, Miss VanCastle, the medical group that performed your surgery does not bill hourly like some lesser establishments."

"No! I wish they would've! It'd probably have been cheaper." I over-explain and argue a little more, but the fight was over before I even made the call. "When I asked about the cost of having my gallbladder removed, you guys told me that while my plan doesn't cover office visits or consultation fees, the operation was covered."

"Yes. And it was."

"Then why do I owe over twenty-five hundred in medical bills?"

"Other fees and expenses."

"That doesn't make any sense!"

"Perhaps you should contact your medical provider for an itemized bill."

There are four bills on my table. The campus doctor, the surgeon, the anesthesiologist, and the hospital. The campus doctor, I understand. My insurance doesn't cover office visits, and I went to an office over a stomach ache. For everything else, I can only imagine this is what drowning feels like. I'm a full time student, living off financial aid. Every semester I receive a check. I budget it to last me until the next one. The added cost of three months' rent all at once is overwhelming. There's no way I can afford all this.

"Have you considered hooking?" Joanie asks. "A good lay can make that kind of money in a single night. It'd probably only take you a few weeks."

"Well...I do need a job," I sigh.

It's Thirsty Thursday and five of us have meandered to Waldo's Tavern, our usual watering hole. The place looks like it belongs on the outskirts of town. All wood. The sort of aesthetic where you'd expect to meet retired, rambling old men. But it's on the edge of campus so the usual crowd consists of boys in fedoras drinking beer while scrolling through memes on their iMacs. I'm not sure it's anyone's favorite hangout, but it is in walking distance, which is appreciated on the days Candace and her friend Kyla decide to start drinking immediately after their last class. The pair were three sheets to the wind when the rest of us arrived. Joanie and Bill are on their first beers while I'm starting the night strong with a Coca-Cola. "I haven't considered sex work specifically," I say. My Coke is a little flat; ever since my surgery I can't enjoy pop without feeling bloated. I really don't care. It's worth it. "I'm only taking thirteen credits this semester, so I'm sure I can find some time, you know, some place. In high school, Dad got me a job doing KP on base. Maybe I could bus tables somewhere."

Joanie and Bill give me a little stink eye. "Holy hell, F-Bomb," Bill says. "Most people go to college so they don't have to wash dishes."

A thing about their nickname for me, F-Bomb, is that it started about three years ago. Maybe I didn't turn out to be the daughter my parents wanted, but they'd at least be pleased to know their bashful little lesbian has never been one for vulgarities. Punked out hair and tattoos sure, but Dad always had a way of pointing out other people's language in public. That's the thing that stuck. Dignity is in the way we address each other, and there is something a little sad about people who say *f this* and *f that* every other sentence. So based entirely on diction, I'm living up to all my parents' hopes and dreams. Except for that one time two years ago when I got a B- on a research paper about microbiomes. In my fury I said, "*Son of a fuck!*" My friends have never let me forget it.

"That could totally be your thing," Joanie says. "You'll do your forensic DNA crap during the day, but then at night you'll make a real difference cleaning plates."

Bill adds he could see me putting on a hairnet the way Batman dons his mask.

Somewhere near the bar, a glass shatters.

Kyla says, "Oh! Better go investigate, F-Bomb! Don't forget your apron and blacklight."

Near the bar, a goth girl holds one beer mug and stares down at the fragments of another. Several people applaud the mess. Everyone else just stares. Except for one man. One enormous bear of a man. He sits in his stool, slouching over his beer and seems oblivious to the world around him. He doesn't react to the broken glass, which is what makes me curious. He doesn't look down at the floor. He doesn't look at the girl. He just sits there, a little too much of the background to be ignored.

"I'm so sorry," the goth girl says to the bartender. "It just slipped. I'll clean it up."

The bartender is a twiggy guy with a blonde afro named Nate. For as long as I've been going to Western, he's the only man I've ever seen tending bar here. I can tell he's annoyed, but he tells the girl, "No worries," as he fills another glass. "Accidents happen. I'll just go grab a broom and a mop. Here. This one's on the house." He gives her a full mug. She apologizes again. She thanks him in a clumsy little conversation. As she starts to walk away, the bear man glances at her legs. He checks her out from the ground up, shrugs, and goes back to his drink. There's something off about the guy. I feel like I know him but can't quite place him.

He doesn't hold my attention for long. Kyla and Candace are planning my vigilante costume between dart throws and it's at least a little funny. "Would she use a tablecloth or some dishrags as a cape?" Candace asks. She tosses a dart and it bounces off the board, stabbing into the floor.

"Ooh. Good question. Which goes better with a pot helmet?" Kyla says, taking her turn to miss the board entirely. "Wait-what's the score?"

"We're keeping score?"

Bill plucks Candace's fallen dart out of the floor and says, "You know it's not even ten and you two are already smashed."

Candace tells him, "Sounds like someone needs to catch up!"

I sigh at nothing in particular and take a sip of my Coke. A few ice cubes slide at my lips. Time for a refill. Thankfully, per usual, Nate doesn't charge me for pop. Even though we always walk here, he still treats me like a designated driver. If I ever do offer to pay, he'll tell me something along the lines of, "Being the responsible one is still being the responsible one. I know who's getting carried out tonight and who's getting everyone home." Who says being a good person doesn't pay? I'll be homeless two months, but hey, at least I'll always have an in for free pop. I'm about to walk over, but-

"Hey, F-Bomb," Joanie whispers from behind me. "Isn't that your girlfriend at the bar?"

Suddenly, I don't want my refill. Wyanet is hoisting herself onto a stool. She's about eight seats away from the bear man, sitting with a backpack and small stack of books.

I watch her with a deer in headlights expression.

"Studying alone at a bar on Thirsty Thursday," Joanie commentates as Wyanet thumbs through her notebook. "Our usual bar. Right when I thought nobody in this world was more helpless or desperate than you."

I'm quick to remind her, "I've studied here plenty of times."

"You're not helping yourself," Joanie says. "But you should definitely go talk to her."

"She's doing homework," I defend her, or myself. Maybe a little of both. "She probably brought the books just to avoid having people flirt with her."

"I've seen you flirt, F-Bomb. I doubt she'll notice."

"Well, that's encouraging."

"You want encouragement? Get nicer friends. In the meantime, the exotic girly who's always on your mind is making a point to be near you again. If she wanted to study, she'd have stayed home or gone to the Rocket Café. When people walk into bars alone, they're hoping for attention. It's a pseudo-scientific fact. The books are an excuse. If you don't go to her, she'll comfort herself in saying she was productive. But if one of you does work up the nerve, well, that'd be something. And it should be."

I sigh. When she puts it like that, she almost sounds sweet.

Candace asks, "What are you two talking about?"

Joanie nods to the bar. "I'm trying to get F-Bomb to go fuck Wyanet."

Candace glances Wyanet's way. After a moment she says, "What's that all about?"

I try to interject, "Will you two stop staring?"

Joanie answers a question with a question. "Will you just go talk to her? You're both such pussies."

"Fine!" I say. "Fine! I mean? Now?"

Joanie rolls her eyes. Candace shakes her head. And I know, *I know*. It's me being myself again. Me making excuses and finding ways to cower. Even the song on the jukebox seems to agree with their expressions. "*Come a little bit closer,*" it sings.

"It's just, you know, she just walked in. I'm thinking I should let her get settled first. Maybe get some studying done. I should at least wait until she takes a break."

"A break could be a single sip of a beer," Joanie says. "A break could be walking out the door and studying at home."

From over my shoulder, Bill hollers, "Grow some balls, Millie!"

Kyla starts laughing. So do a few other people. Including the bear man, which means there's no way Wyanet didn't hear it. So that feels a lot less than perfect.

"Fine," I say. "I'll um, I'll go say, 'Hi!' I'll say that if she feels like taking a break, she's welcome to come join or us. How's that?"

Joanie pats me on the shoulder and says, "Great. Whatever. Just make sure you emphasize the word *come.*" She shoves me in the direction of the bar and smacks me on the butt. I stumble. I nearly lose my glass of ice. As I rebalance, I give a not so subtle gesture with my middle finger, pretending to scratch the back of my head.

"F-Bomb!" they all scream and no doubt take a shot of their drinks. That's the tradition developed over the past few years. They play the world's soberest drinking game. If I ever curse, everybody takes a drink. It's such a rare event; I don't see the point. But it doesn't stop them. It's one more way to tease their meek friend, and for that, they love it.

The jukebox continues to sing. "*Come a little bit closer. I'm all alone. And the night is so long.*" I think the band is Jay & The Americans. It's one of the songs the jukebox always seems to have cued when nobody selects something for a while. I try to distract myself remembering the title.

It doesn't work. What did I just agree to? I'm thirty steps to the bar and my heart is pounding. I take a deep, calming breath. It doesn't help. Memories of the last time we spoke are stabbing me. Not when she gave up. Two weeks later when I tried to win her back. When she said I made her feel so alone. Standing on her porch, in that green tank top I'd bought her a year before, she told me that I never stop leaving her behind. And now I'm supposed to walk up and talk to her. Like, "Oh hey! I feel like less and less of a woman every day. How've you been?"

The best possible conversation right now is if I was to walk up and she smacks me across the face with one of her textbooks, then goes back to studying like nothing ever happened. It's painful. Definitive. And less frightening than trying to talk.

A thing about Wyanet is…there are too many things about Wyanet.

Over the summer I concluded things aren't meant to work out with your first love. Specifically because it's your first love. It's your purest, most romanticized relationship. The one you try to make live up to all the happily ever afters while being so horribly unequipped for the needs of another person. You need to be shattered a few times and glued back together, leaving your fragments of ideals on the floor.

We started dating my sophomore year, just before Mama told me Dad died. We'd met next door at Rocket Café, through Joanie. They were partners on some project. Joanie ended up doing most of the work because I kept inviting myself along to their study sessions. We joked. We teased. We both danced around asking each other out. Like two mice scampering around a piece of cheese, too scared to bite because what if it's a trap?

I don't know if it's wrong of me, but I think I had an easier time with Dad's death because of puppy love. I found out in the middle of our second date. Mama called to tell me he'd had cancer, died, and the funeral was lovely. Wyanet held me the rest of the night, letting me oscillate between anger and grief. She was always so easy to be vulnerable around. Which is half the reason I don't want to talk to her now.

Sometimes, anxiety can taste like french fries and vomit. Wyanet's black hair catches the gleam of blue light from a Budweiser sign. Her polo hugs her shoulders and I remember how comfortably my head could rest right there. She turns a little, to watch Nate pass by with a mop and bucket. She blinks and I remember what it's like waking up to those eyes three inches from me. She sees me. Oh god. God damn it. She sees me.

"*Come a little bit closer...*"

Our eyes meet and the entire universe slows to a crawl. She smiles, tender and easy like the sunrise. Just as her familiar warmth drapes over me, our moment is murdered in the trumpet of a fart.

The bear man shifts in his seat. His grimy flannel lifts enough to reveal a glistening tuft of hair in his butt crack. It's like a squirrel chose the top of his jeans as a suitable place to die. I pointedly direct my eyes away, back to Wyanet's. But it's too late. I've seen everything. The image will remain a part of me for the rest of my life.

"Hiya, Millie," Nate says, sweeping wet glass into a dustbin. He's squinting, his entire face shrivelling in defense of bad gas. "Need a refill?"

"Sure, but take your time," I say. Although he has the glass pretty well swept up, he hasn't begun to mop.

"It's no problem," he says, leaning the broom against the bar, next to his mop bucket.

I choose a stool two away from Wyanet. I rest my hands on the bar. They're trembling just a little.

Nate asks, "Was it Coke or Cherry Coke tonight?"

"Regular, but cherry sounds good," I say. I watch Wyanet and she watches back. The bear man's fart hits me. I do my best to ignore it.

While Nate fills my glass he says, "How about you, Wyanet? Haven't seen you here in awhile. I have some of your dad's Cabaret in."

"My fridge is full of it," she says. "How about a Pinot Noir?"

"Black Star Farms?"

"That's a good one."

Everything seems to linger. Wyanet's soft smile. Her eyes. The song on the jukebox. The bear man's stench. It's like sulfur and eggs in a puddle of mustard. I'm trying not to notice, to focus on my ex, to find the right words, but dear god, how are we all still alive under this stink? How has it not passed? I wave my hand over my nose and Wyanet plugs hers. She giggles. I can't help but join her. If there was ever an ice breaker, this fart just melted the polar continents.

Wyanet speaks first. *Thank God.* "Do you still use that peach-strawberry shampoo?"

"I'm out. I've been using Candace's… whatever it is."

"Either way, how about you sit a bit closer?"

I scramble to scoot to the next stool. It feels like I just fell for a pick up line. I'm tempted to ask, "Why are you here?" But I don't. I just watch her golden brown eyes. If my heart had its own consciousness, it'd be acutely aware of the scar beneath my ribs. It'd be thinking, *if the gallbladder can be ripped out that way, then so can I!* It's been six months. Six months since she gave up on me.

Wyanet says, "That's not helping, but thanks. I've been..." She trails off. The air is so heavy with the thick stench of fart. "I've been wanting to talk to you," she says fully this time. Definitively.

"Oh?" I say. My heart starts to scramble. It pushes against my scar, looking frantically around for something sharp to ease its escape. Perhaps some discarded scalpel left over from my surgery.

Talking to Wyanet was a terrible idea. I should've stayed away. I should've just stayed with my friends and helped them plan my vigilante dishwasher costume. At best this is a 'let's be friends,' conversation, to which the answer is no. No. *Not in a million years*. I'm nowhere near over you and nothing in this world can make me pretend a friendship with you would be easy.

"I don't like how I left things between us," she says. And it's clear. She just wants to make peace. I can feel it. "I didn't mean to…"

I cut her off. I tell her it's okay. "If anybody should feel guilty here, it's me. I held back too much. Like, all the time." Dear God, I'm absolutely going to end this conversation by saying we can be friends and giving her a hug. Now I'm not even sure if it's the gas in the air or just me feeling like a fart.

She says, "I miss you."

Somewhere deep within me, my heart holds a wedge of sharpened plaque up over its aorta, about to shank its escape. Her words give it pause. In reality, the feeling is expressed through a deer-in-headlights stare.

The fart bag makes some noise from his other end. "You just drinkin' a soda?" His voice is somewhere between rolling thunder and a car horn. "Somebody not tell ya this here's a bar or somethin'?"

The bear man is eyeing me with all his enormity. Even with him sitting, slouched over, I have to look up to meet his gaze. One eye is bloodshot, squinting just a little. It's not pink or dried out. More like half the vessels in his sclera exploded. Maybe it's just the light in here, but the blood seems to churn, or fold over itself. It's freaky enough that I look away. Not to be rude. I look just below his eyes instead of directly at them. His face is weathered and sunburned. Several scars streak like comets into his full beard. The top of his head is the only hairless part of him. His bald scalp practically glows. He bites his lip as he stares me down, absently picking at chapped skin.

"I uh, I don't drink," I try to brush him off. I turn back to Wyanet. "You miss-?"

The bear man says, "Leaves more for me," like he doesn't care but wants everybody in the room to know he doesn't care. "Though yer missin' out on a helluva a beer. Bartender, what's this watered down piss called again?"

Nate says, "It's a local brew. *Battle Draught*. You liking it?"

"I had better n' m'day," The bear man nods. "But it ain't been my day in fuckin' forever. It's perty damn good ta tell the truth. Another round fer me n' this sober l'il girly here."

"Oh, no thank you," I say. "Really, I don't drink. I can't. It makes me ill." Wyanet is just as frozen as me. She's annoyed, but what do you do?

"That an excuse or did I just hear some air escape yer pussy?" the bear man says. "Tell ya what. I'll make a wager. You was with them trampy girls all the way o'er by them dartboards, right? I'll betcha I can get myself a bullseye on that board, from here, in a single shot."

"I'm sorry?" I say. "Did you just say air escape from my…"

"If I make it, ya'll gotta at least taste one sip o' this damn fine Battle Draught I'm drinkin' here. If I miss, I'll buy you your soda."

"No. I need you to stop talking. You need to get away from me. Now." I say.

Nate comes to my rescue. He says, "I don't think the lady is interested, sir."

"I can assess that fer m'self," the bear man says. "An' I ain't askin' 'er fer a date. I'm jus' enjoyin' this here Battle Daught, but enjoyin' it alone. Kind of a sad picture, don'cha think? So I'm making a bet. Jus' a harmless li'l bet. But if she won' take it, maybe 'er li'l injun friend will." He looks to Wyanet. "What breed are ya down there, Missy? Pottawatomie?"

Wyanet perks up. "How could you tell?"

"Injuns all got their own smell. Kinda like how virgins all smell a certain way. To the acute nose, so do all the human, uh, whate'er they're called. Sub-species, I s'pose."

"Excuse me?" She says.

"Excuse me?" I say. "What did you just call her?"

"Hm?" The bear man shrugs. "Nothin'. Jus' called her like I saw her. Perty sure I'm right 'bout you too, ain't I?"

I sit a little straighter. "Do you have any idea how rude you're being right now?"

He looks around to Nate and Wyanet, with a somewhat baffled expression. He looks at them like I'm some sort of crazy. "I'm jus' enjoying a drink. So whadaya say, Injun girl? I score a bullseye n' you share a beer with me?"

That tears it. I can't stand the thought of him speaking to Wyanet for another second. So instead of letting her answer I say, "How about this bet. You make your shot, from here, one chance, and I'll buy you a damn pitcher-"

"F-Bomb!" my friends scream from across the room. They all lift their glasses and drink.

I start again, "I'll buy a stupid pitcher of your stupid beer. You miss the bullseye, and you leave. Either way, you apologize to her and the rest of us for your backwoods tongue and learn to be a bit more civil in the future."

The entire bar is silent. I don't take my eyes off him, but I can feel the room watching us. What just happened? That's not like me. I don't get aggressive like this.

The bear man stands. His height is startling but I don't show him how intimidated I am. Not for a second. I stare hard into his disgusting bloodshot eye and refuse to blink.

"The name's Gus Beauregard," he says.

"Millie VanCastle."

"Millie," he nods. "It's a fuckin' pleasure." He brushes his flannel aside, reaching under the sleeve like he's going for a gun. The T-shirt he's wearing beneath states in bold, black capitals, *I FUCK SHEEP*. His hand emerges from his flannel with a machete. He doesn't break eye contact. He doesn't blink. He just arches the knife over his head and throws.

The song continues to play. "*Man you know you're in trouble plenty.*"

The blade gleams in the air, spinning across the room. It flies past Joanie, past Bill, right between Candace and Kyla's glasses as they're about to clink, and stabs deep into the absolute dead center of the bullseye.

Gus doesn't have to look to know he made his shot. He just gives me a dirty little wink.

Somebody, some guy in the room yells, "Holy shit!" and the entire place breaks into applause. Somebody else yells out, "Do it again!"

"Get m'knife," Gus yells back. Then to Wyanet he nods and says, "Ma'am. I don' know how I offended you, but I always been blessed with a coarse way about m'words. The presence of ladies is still regarded fer whatever fucking reason. Fer my failure to appreciate that, I do apologize."

Wyanet rolls her eyes. "It's okay. Good throw."

Gus shrugs. "'Twas fer booze." To me, he says, "No hard feelin's, I hope."

"You really think you're something," I say. It feels like a con. He swindled me. I just can't figure out how.

The song plays, "*You're my kind of man.*"

He says, "I know what I am. How about that beer? Not to interrupt yer little powwow with the natives, but ya owe me a drink. Of course yer welcome ta share it."

I'm not in a compromising mood. "I'll stick with Coke," I tell him, starting to realize I made a bet, and I owe this ridiculously enormous man a pitcher of beer. With money. Money I don't have. I need to ask Joanie and Candace. Great. "I'll just get some cash for that pitcher." I take two steps away from the bar and there's some guy approaching with Gus's machete. "Hey, man," he says. "I got your sword!" He's clearly a little tipsy, and fakes a throwing motion. As his arm comes forward, he slips on the beer puddle. His entire body jolts. His jaw drops. The machete slides from his hand. As it arcs in the air, my reflexes are fast enough to linger onto a thought, "That's not a sword."

"So big and so strong!"

I'm significantly faster to react when the machete stabs my thigh. That is to say, I drop to the floor, screaming at the top of my lungs because oh my god, oh my god, oh my god there's a machete in my leg!

"Come a little bit closer!"

The first one over me is Gus. "Hurry! He says. "We gotta ri'se the wound!" He lifts my leg and rolls the mop bucket beneath it. "Now we gotta tie it off. Slow the bleedin'!" He's quick to tear the sleeve off my shirt and ties it around my thigh, just above the machete. "Somebody bring some fuckin' towels!" He yells. "Somebody call that there nine-nine-nine!"

"Come a little bit closer, I'm all alone."

In my writhing, I try to grab for the machete's handle. Gus presses down on my chest and snaps, "No! Don' remove it. You'll bleed out. We need ta put pressure o'er it." He rips the front of my shirt clean off and bunches it, making bundles around where blade meets leg. I cover myself as best I can. Even in agony, it doesn't take long to realize my comfy bra is exposed to the world. My oldest bra. The most worn down, broken in piece of clothing I own that looks better suited for a dumpster than a person. The bra Wyanet suggested I throw out on more than one occasion. Or to quote, "If you have to wear it, can we at least go to a rally where there's a chance you'll end up burning it."

While I multitask contemplating both shreds of my vanity while violently thrashing around, Joanie is screaming at Gus. "What are you doing?" she says. The veins on her neck throb.

"Savin' her life!" Gus snaps back.

"Why didn't you use your shirt?"

Gus, still holding my leg, glances at his flannel, then back at Joanie. He shrugs, "Fer what? Where the hell's them towels?"

Nate throws some dishrags over the counter. "Here!" He says. "They're clean!"

"Keep 'em comin'!" Gus yells. "Keep 'em comin'!"

So here I am, flailing on the floor, crying, screaming in a worn out bra, with a machete sticking out of my leg as a jukebox belts out, "*Closer! Closer! Closer!*" Gus and Joanie continue to argue. When I notice Wyanet, it occurs that my head is resting on her knees. She's holding my shoulder down with one hand and stroking my forehead with the other. She's whispering something I can't hear over the other voices. I want to ask her in a cheesy cute sort of way, "So you really miss me?" But it comes out more like, "Oh my god! Take it out! Please just take the knife out! Please! Dear God!"

Things pretty much stay that way until the ambulance arrives. From there it's paramedics, more bandages, and an ever darkening, fading world. I really don't know if I black out from the pain or blood loss. Probably a combination of both. The last thing I remember hearing is something of a conversation between Joanie and Nate.

"Where did that guy go?" Joanie asks.

Nate says, "Where's my mop bucket?"

Somewhere in the calamity I want to write Mama a letter. *Dear Mama, I miss you and I hate it. I get mad at myself sometimes wondering if you're okay. Love, Millie*

I wake up in a hospital bed with Joanie holding my hand. "Remember all those times we gave blood?" She says. "Well, you got some back! Who knows. Probably not your own, but maybe. Think of it like a rebate." I ask her what happened to my clothes and she says, "They had to cut off everything near the wound. The only piece of clothing that survived was your bra, and from the look of it I'd say that died years ago. Candace went home to get you some things, but it's been a few hours. I'm pretty sure she's sleeping one off."

After a while she asks how my face feels. I tell her it's fine but question why. She shrugs. "No reason. How are you otherwise?"

The face question gives me pause, but I let it go. "Kind of devastated. Wyanet said she misses me."

"Oh?" Joanie's eyebrows perk up. The bead on her piercing slides down. "I was talking about your leg."

The doctor is unsure if the machete did any permanent damage. She tells me, "The blade cut through a lot of tissue, but you seem to have full functionality of your foot. There's a lot we can't tell right now, but I'm hopeful. It's too early, but physical therapy is a safe bet in your future."

They give me my comfy bra back in a yellow, plastic bag with a biohazard symbol on it. I sigh. I don't know if that's standard practice or a subtle message from the hospital staff.

The discharge nurse says I can expect a bill in the mail. I don't ask for how much. I try to tell myself that money comes and goes, so who cares? This is just another adventure on the road of life. Yesterday, I never would've expected to end up in crutches while nursing a machete wound. That's exciting, right? I try to tell myself you can't put a price on excitement.

It doesn't work.

Candace brings me fresh clothes and takes me home in a cab. During the drive she asks if my nose is okay, and I question why everybody keeps asking about my face. She looks at me a long moment and tells the driver to take the next right. As we pull into the parking lot I ask again, but she hops out of the car to get my door. As I fumble with my crutches she changes the subject. "Do you smell something?"

"It's not me, is it? I'm sure I stink like hospital bed. How am I supposed to bathe with all these bandages on?"

"Not you," she says. "I mean, you're right. You need a shower. But it's like barbeque almost, with something…" she trails off.

I sniff the air. "Oh! What is that? Want to track it down and bring me back a plate?"

"Yeah, I could go walking around all over the place and flirt my way into a free plate," she says. "Or we could call Joanie and Kyla and have them pick up Chinese."

I'm sway on my crutches. Hunger hasn't occurred to me until just now. When was the last time I ate? Although the barbeque smells phenomenal, the crab rangoon from Campus Kitchen is to die for. And I haven't had any since my gallbladder was removed. Maybe I can eat it again without all the pain afterward. "Well, I guess I did earn some cashew chicken. Did you hear I got stabbed by a machete?"

Candace says, "The entire town heard the moment you got stabbed by the machete."

I'm supposed to make sure I keep the bandages dry for at least the next twenty four hours. The only cleaning up I do is performed over the sink. I'm able to wash my face and hands. Somehow blood got into my hair, but I'm able to rinse it out with at least a little success. For all the good it does, I splash water around and pat myself dry. I give myself a quick look over in the mirror, staring at the dressing around my leg. For no reason in particular it makes me think of Dad.

In all his years as a soldier, I wonder if he'd picked up any scars like the one I just had carved into me. I think to call Mama, to tell her what happened. But as soon as the thought enters, I hesitate. It's been years now. Even if I had it in myself to call home, the last thing I want to discuss is how I got stabbed and am now even more broke than ever. Of course I'd have to mention the gallbladder surgery. And the fact that I'm still not attracted to men. Also my political views are leaning closer to the left and I really wish they hadn't fed me so much red meat growing up. I have a hard time imagining my mom's reactions. Would she call me Sweetie like she used to? Or Emmeline? Would she be worried? Or even care? The more I think about it the more I imagine her silence. Or if she does decide to chat, I picture her uttering, "Okay. Okay. Okay," until it's time to hang up. Phrases like *good bye*, *I miss you*, and especially *I love you* feel are unlikely at best.

I decide against the call.

However I do decide on plaid pajama pants and a baggy army t-shirt I've had since I was a kid. Dressed, alone in my room, I tear open the seal of the biohazard bag and toss my comfy bra into a hamper. It's not *that* bloodstained.

Candace emerges from her bedroom and peers into mine. She says, "You're wearing that?"

"What?"

"Nothing," she says. "Nothing. It's just, maybe you'd like to put on something a little nicer."

"For staying in and cheap Chinese food?"

Candace hesitates. After a moment she says, "I know, but it's a little early for pajamas, isn't it?"

"I'm nursing a stab wound. I got stabbed."

"Yeah," she says. "Yeah! Of course. You're right. You just got out of the hospital. I'm going to get in the shower. The door is unlocked, so don't worry about getting up for anybody."

"I have no intention of it," I say. I fumble around my bedroom until I find a book of crosswords and crutch my way back to the living room.

Again, Candace looks me over. "Maybe you want to at least put on a tank top? Or! Hey, I found the best lipstick this afternoon. How about a little makeover?"

"You know I don't wear... Did you say *this afternoon*? Did you go shopping while I was waiting at the hospital?"

Her smile ignites like a flash bomb. "*Prior*. I meant *prior* afternoon. Anyway, you're right. Not your thing. Maybe I'll win you over some day. I'm going to get in the shower before Kyla gets here."

"Okay?" I say. She's acting funny. Not just with the cute deflection, but something is going on with her. Then again, I've spent the better part of the day being told to wiggle my toes, so my normalcy gauge is probably a bit off. I crutch my way over to the couch and nestle in for some intense crossword action. As I get settled, I try putting my leg up. I bend my knee a little. It doesn't go far, and hurts to no end. The doctors had prescribed me a pretty large dose of Tylenol, but I don't think I can take any for a few more hours. So instead I try not to think about it. I open my book to a random page and dive into the first clue I see.

Bradbury and Shakespeare's What Comes This Way.

In fifteen empty spaces I write *SOMETHINGWICKED.*

It must've been a slow day at the crossword factory because in fifteen breezy minutes I have the puzzle almost entirely filled out. I'm just about to write in *Caligula* when there's a thumping at my door.

"Come in," I yell. "It's open."

After a moment, another thump. Not a knock. A thump.

"The door's open, Kyla!" I know it's Kyla because Joanie would've tried walking in before considering to knock.

Another thump.

Whatever the problem is, Kyla isn't even trying. I hoist myself up and announce again, "It's open. Come on in," to no answer. I crutch my way around the sofa, into the hall. "Come in," I call again, and again the door doesn't budge. So I open it, see Wyanet standing on my stoop, scream, and slam the door shut.

For a few seconds, the only sound is from the shower in the bathroom.

I look down at myself and realize why Candace had been wanting me to put on some nicer clothes.

The door thumps. It's her foot.

I open the door and stare, petrified at the sight of golden eyes and raven black hair. "Wyanet?"

She's standing here like a dream. A dream with two arms full of carryout Chinese. "May I come in?" she asks, a sense of urgency in her tone. "The bag started to rip on the bottom."

"I'm so sorry!" I say.

"I'm sorry I startled you, but really, we're about to get fried cat meat all over the place."

I crutch back a couple of steps and my heel bops the wall, which shoots a pain up my thigh. I wince, but ignore the sudden throbbing. "Come in. I'm so, so sorry!"

Wyanet walks straight to the kitchen portion and sets both bags on the counter. It's been months and she finds her way around like it was yesterday. She knows exactly where to find plates. The silverware. She digs under the forks until she comes up with two pairs of the stainless steel chopsticks she gave me forever ago. She knows enough to look around and say, "Did Candace move out? Everything looks so clean."

I fumble. The crutches are still awkward. I wasn't prepared to use them while being self conscious. "She cleaned. She thought I'd have trouble navigating around 'her areas.'"

"Oh. You should get injured more often."

I don't have anything to add. I watch as she plates our food. She divides the rangoons between us, scoops out two spoonfuls of white rice for me and one for her. It's like some old home video is playing. Like she left us on pause for the summer and just randomly hit play again.

She starts toward the couch with both plates but halts to look me over. "I'm sorry. Do you, um-this was a bad idea. Do you want me to leave?"

I shake my head and blink a time or two, but whatever part of me that knew how to speak is glitching. "I'm," I start to say but pause before I vomit out any number of baffled obscenities. I go with, "Surprised." Hopefully not sounding too much like I'm on a lot of pain killers, "but delighted."

The bathroom door opens and Candace walks out in platform heels, a black skirt, a sequined sapphire tank top, and glittery blue eye shadow. "Oh look," she says, her tone playfully bored. "Wyanet is here to talk things over. Well, I'm going out dancing with Kyla, so I'll probably crash on her couch. You girls have fun." She walks out into the world, locking the door behind her.

I gulp.

We eat. Well, I go through the motions of stabbing cashew chicken with a fork, sticking it in my mouth, chewing, swallowing, and repeating the process at a slow pace while staring at my plate and being all too aware of the beautiful, devastating, and perfect woman who broke my heart as she sits relatively near me on the sofa. So everything I'm busying myself with looks an awful like eating. Mostly it's an elaborate method of avoiding eye contact. It's me accepting that, yes, there is a massive elephant in the room. But as long as I continue to graze, the elephant is safely behind a houseplant and therefore not quite as visible.

Wyanet says, "Is this a mistake?"

So much for houseplants.

I don't put the next broccoli floret in my mouth. It lingers on my fork, two inches from my face. A glob of brown sauce is stuck to its side, hanging somewhere between self-sacrifice and the denial of gravity. I don't eat it. I can't put another thing in my mouth. But I still swallow. "You said you missed me."

She drops her hand the way she drops her hand when she's at a loss for words. Immediately, I'm annoyed. I don't say it. I don't express it. I just know the motion. The stammered expression. If she sighs, I've said something wrong and there's an argument in the making. If she doesn't, I've said something wrong and she's working on a defense. Either way, I've broken a dam and built a wall. Six months and I can still find all her buttons without so much as looking.

"I'm sorry," she says. "I shouldn't have come here. I don't know what I was thinking."

I want to tell her, "Clearly. It's been months and if not for that one class, I was just starting to get used to you not being around. I was just starting to move on. And now you're here to what? To remind me of what it feels like to have my heart ripped out? To pretend like the past is the past and just move on like old friends? Like in the end you weren't frustrated with how indecisive I am? Like you always felt like we weren't going anywhere because I wasn't going anywhere? Do you know how crippling that is? To be left feeling like all I ever did was hold you back? Like I'm not worth your love? And now, what? You miss me? How? Miss me like a friend? Miss our relationship? Miss me like the anchor who always kept you from getting anywhere?" In my heart, I say all of that.

But...God, I hate how much I love her being on my couch. So out loud, for the second time in twenty-four hours, I give in. "I'm glad to see you," I say-mean. Or at least I think I mean. "I just don't understand. What changed?"

Her gaze fixes on me, so my gaze shifts to my food. She says, "You weren't there. I know how terrible this sounds, but a few weeks went by and I was still missing you. I dated a little. I tried meeting people. I was moving on, but I also couldn't. Does that make sense?" I don't answer. I just let her ramble. "I think a lot of us breaking up was…you know how we all have our expectations of what love is? Or what it should be? I've had a lot of time to think about this. A lot more than I can probably get out in a single explanation. But I think a lot of the time, those last few months, I was coming up with excuses. I started picking and over analyzing everything. *This is what a relationship should look like.* Ours never fit the model. You're not that idealized person. That doesn't sound right. What I mean is, I couldn't see what I had because I was too focused on what I thought I was missing. So I turned you into a ball and chain. I turned our relationship into a prison. So I left. Then I kept missing you. Then I couldn't believe you were still in that class. I was so sure you would've dropped."

"I tried. Everything else was booked up. So I talked Joanie into coming. Honestly, I thought you would've dropped it too." In the back of my mind, I'm thinking about how she called me a *ball and chain.* One, that's horrible. Two, why didn't I think of that instead of anchors?

She chuckles. "Yeah. I had the same problem. But I'm glad it worked out that way. I get to see you and it reaffirms everything I've been feeling. You're gone after class, and my heart sinks. My favorite part of the week is over."

Oh God. She's good. None of that should've worked, but it all does.

"Of course, I finally worked up the nerve to tell you all this, and as soon as we start talking, everything smells like fart and you end up with a sword in your leg."

What do I say to this? Yes, I miss her. Yes, I'm miserable. But she left. I can barely process her explanation, and it's sinking in that she has no clue where my life is. I need a job. I'm broke. My gallbladder is gone, which means I'm literally less of a person than I was when she left. "You hurt me," I tell her. "It's not like my life stopped and I was left waiting for the moment where you return with really good Chinese food."

"I don't expect you to forgive me," she says. "I don't blame you for not giving me a second chance. I just spent a lot of time thinking about it, and I wanted to tell you. After what happened last night, I think I probably would've held off, but Candace and Kyla kept telling me to come over."

"You've been talking to Candace and Kyla?"

"A bit. I drove them to the hospital last night. Your friends were really, really wasted. After Candace fell on your head, flirting with that paramedic, I figured I should be the one driving."

That explains the nose. "Oh. Well, thanks. That actually clears up a few things." I fall silent. It's too much to process. I honestly have no idea if it's the situation or the painkillers that have me feeling off. So I let the elephant sit. I admire the houseplant. I breathe. A bit of time passes and I start to feel anxious about how much time I'm letting pass. She's watching me. She's waiting for my reply. I tell her, "I think I need to let this sink in."

"Oh," she sinks a little herself. "Do you want me to go?"

In my heart I say, "No." But then aloud I tell her, "Yes. But… if you wanted to ask me out next week, I'd probably only say *no* to dancing."

She smirks. "So bowling then?"

God. That worked too.

She takes me to a movie. I wait outside the theater while Wyanet parks the car. I've never been here before, but I like the classic look of the place. It's a brown brick building with a marquee overlooking a booth. An older man sits behind the window, dapper in his bow tie and little hat.

Wyanet was telling me on the way over they play second run movies, art films, and indie flicks. We're not even sure what's playing. She knows movies usually started around seven and we have time. So I agree to a movie and -maybe- a late dinner. If things went well. Whoever I was kidding. Of course I'd agree to dinner. As soon as she'd opened my door at the car-as soon as she held my crutches while I eased in and buckled-I'd agree to anything she wanted.

But I have to hold back. Or at least tell myself I'm playing it safe. She left me. For all I know she might snap out of this newfound longing and leave me again. She might not even be parking the car right now. She's probably driving home, relieved to have dodged a bullet and left me waiting on the sidewalk. I grow anxious as I wait. A minute passes. One minute turns into two minutes. Who takes two minutes to park a car?

I breathe. I'm being weird. I need to relax. It's just a date. I decide to figure out what movie we'll be watching. I take a closer look around the old man in the booth, looking for a poster or title with times written. Instead, something else catches my eye. A help wanted sign.

The man notices me staring and through the little holes in the window he says, "Can I help you?"

I crutch over a few steps and ask, "What are you hiring for?"

"Whatever I can get," he shrugs. "Problem with running a business in a college town. You gain and lose employees at the drop of a hat."

"Do you have an application?" I ask. "And is walking a necessity of the job?"

The old man leans forward and looks me over through the window. I'm wearing some baggy jeans, so the bandages are covered, but I'm still keeping my leg suspended. Maybe letting my crutches support me a little more than usual. "What happened to you there, Missy?" He's close enough that I can read his nametag. *Wilbur Post.*

"Um," I don't know why but I try to think of something more plausible than what actually happened. In the end I can't bring myself to lie. "A drunk guy dropped a machete on my leg."

He continues staring with a quizzical look in his eye. Taking a deep breath through his nose and scratches the stubble on his chin. "You ever run a cash register before?" he asks.

"No," I say. "But I'm good with numbers. I've been balancing my checkbook for years."

"You old enough for a checkbook?"

"I'm twenty-one!"

"Alright. Just teasing. Say I hire you. Any drunken machete wielding boyfriends going to be coming around here?"

Right then, Wyanet comes walking up from behind me. She places her hand on the small of my back. "What are we seeing?" she asks.

I blush a little. In front of Mister Post, interviewing me on the spot, Wyanet's timing is probably a little less than professional. Between their two questions, I decide to answer Post's first. "Definitely not," I say.

He seems to put two and two together. He scratches beneath his chin again and says, "You got a name, Missy?"

"Millie," I smile, "Mille VanCastle."

Post nods, "All right. Tell you what, Miss VanCastle. You two ladies go enjoy your movie and have a good evening. You call or come by the theater Tuesday and I'll see about setting you up in the ticket booth."

"Really?" I say, probably a little louder than appropriate. "Thank you, Mister Post! You won't regret it."

"*Post*?" He utters, but then smiles and seems to be holding back a laugh. "Ah. Yes. Well, we'll discuss that too. You have a good evening now."

And I do. The movie is something about colorblind bounty hunter who falls for the woman he's after. I don't pay as much attention to the screen as I do the feeling of the girl beside me. After the film we go to a Tapas place. I listen to her ramble about her dad experimenting with new white wines at his vineyard. I watch her rake her fingers through her hair and it has that same newness and familiarity of spending time with someone in a dream. Maybe I'd feel different without the prospect of a new job. Or it's just something in the air. Neither of us really changed in six months, and on any other day I'd be having a breakdown, straining to smile while inside thinking, "*oh my God, six months. Six months! Here she is and I haven't changed one iota in six months*." Sure, the thought is there. But it's easy. I don't let it win.

By the time we get to my door, all my usual uncertainties are small enough to let me give her a goodnight kiss. Her familiar flavor of Burts Bees lip balm is enough to let her follow me in. Of course I ruin the moment. My crutch lands on a shoe. I slip. I don't fall, but my moment of flailing into a stiff brace is enough to murder any sense of sensuality.

She giggles. With just a little sass she says, "Yep. Still my Millie."

"That's what I get for leaving the lights off."

Her fingertips graze my shoulder as she moves through the dark. She guides me to the sofa, lies me down, and drapes herself over me.

If there's any sort of world beyond her, I wouldn't know a thing about it.

"I swear somebody's been cooking ribs the past three days," Mister Post tells me as he lets me into the theater. "It's been driving me insane. Did some restaurant open? I haven't heard nothing."

I try to shrug while I crutch into the lobby, but the two motions don't work together so instead I probably look more like a chicken clucking along. "There seems to be a lot of that," I say. "My roommate and girlfriend were both talking about how they could smell barbeque." It occurs to me that I just referred to Wyanet as my girlfriend. I didn't mean to, but the word slipped so naturally. Out of nowhere I start wondering if I should've even used it in front of Mister Post like that. He didn't seem taken aback the other night, but the subject of my sexuality, particularly around older people, is still touchy. Even after several years, I flashback to my parents...to the last time I saw my dad alive. It's always such a challenge to think other people might react different.

Despite my uncertainty, Mister Post doesn't seem to notice. He walks ahead of me, slow and seemingly without direction. "The uniform here is simple," he says. "White button up shirt, black slacks. Boys and girls alike. I don't allow skirts, but given your condition I can make an exception."

I smile. As far as job interviews go, this is going well. At least, I've never heard of a job interview opening with a dress code. I'm quick to say, "I don't think I even own a skirt." As I say it, I do recall a sundress or two that may be in my closet. I might have donated them last summer.

"Really?" Mister Post pauses. "To each his own, I suppose. I do recommend it though. There's nothing quite like a summer breeze between your thighs." After an awkward bit of silence, he continues. "Of course, the rest of your uniform you'll keep here, just in here." He takes several more steps to the side of the lobby and opens a door. It's a small closet inside, with just a single bar of red vests on hangers. The last hanger on the right holds a plastic grocery bag full of bow ties. Above them is a shelf of little red bellhop hats. "I used to let the staff take these home, but they'd lose them. If that happens, it's twenty dollars out of a paycheck, and nobody likes that. So first thing you do when you get here is put on your uniform." He reaches into the plastic bag and pulls out a bowtie. "They're pre-tied, so no worries in learning how to tie one. You get your choice of black and red. First thing you do is put all this on. Then the last thing you do before we leave is take it off and keep it here. Think you can handle that?"

I nod. "If not, there's something severely wrong with me."

He smiles. "You'd be surprised. Some of the people who've wandered through here over the years… I'll tell you." He rolls his eyes. "Well, Jesus doesn't care much for me speaking against others, so I'll leave it at that. Most of the job I can teach you once your leg heals. Until then, I'm keeping you in the front lines. You ever work a ticket booth before?"

We walk back across the lobby and he opens a door between the entrance and exit. Inside is a little glass booth with a single stool and a cash register. "Go on," he says. "Have a seat. I'll show you how it works."

I crutch inside. There's hardly any room, but I manage my way onto the stool and lean my crutches against the doorframe.

"Good!" he says, then shuts the door. A moment later he appears outside and taps the window between us. "This stuff's bulletproof, you know. Ain't never had a problem in this neighborhood, but my last theater, back in the days, had a couple stick ups. So I don't take chances. You hear me in there, all right?"

His voice is muffled somewhat from the windows, but I can hear him just fine and say as much.

"Well, that's half the job right there," he tells me. "The other half," he trails off, pulling a five dollar bill out of his pocket. "Is right here." He steps forward and says, "One please." He slides the bill through a partition under the window.

I look at it, then up to him.

He looks at me puzzled for a moment, then says, "Well your first step is to take the five dollars."

I tap one finger onto the five and slide it the rest of the way in.

"That right there is the exact price of one movie ticket. Three dollars if we're showing something second run. If you look just below the counter, you've got two drawers. Go ahead and open those."

I open them. The one on top is a cash drawer, already filled with a number of singles, fives, tens. The drawer beneath it is deeper and holds spools of red, blue, and yellow raffle tickets.

"Once you've gotten the money, you give the customer the desired amount of tickets. Simple as that. Go ahead and show me you can get through the motions."

I blink a couple of times and adjust my glasses. I slide the five into the cash drawer and then start to tear a ticket from the red spool. Then I stop. "Is there a difference in the color coding."

"Sure is!" Mister Post nods. "Well, not much of one. Just pick a color for the current show and stick with that color. Then don't repeat that color for the rest of the night."

"I can do that," I nod.

"I'd worry if you couldn't. So I suppose that leaves just three questions and some tax purpose paperwork to fill out."

"Okay," I can't help but grin. *I just got a job!*

"Are you sure about the machete wielding boyfriends? I run a respectable business and I don't need that sort of folk coming around here."

"Positive," I smile. He must not have picked up on my comment about Wyanet before, so I spell it out for him with, "I'm gay."

"All right then," he says. "Do you own a button up, white shirt and black slacks? Oh, and black shoes while we're on the subject."

"All three."

"And when are you available to start?"

"Tomorrow?" Joanie repeats as I slide into her passenger seat. "I had to go through three interviews and a drug test before I got my job."

I tell her, "I remember. You used my pee. And this isn't exactly daycare. The job is literally sitting in a booth for six hours. I have to stay there the whole time, but there's a little intercom between myself and the refreshment counter, so if I need a break, snack or anything, I can just call. He even told me I can bring homework or something to read. Just nothing that makes noise, and I have to keep it below the counter."

"Can you keep Wyanet down there?"

"What?"

"All the way down there?"

My face gets hot. I'd jab her with my crutch, but there isn't enough room in the car.

The next day, I arrive at the theater early and meet a couple of my coworkers. "They'll handle concessions," Mister Post says. He ushers me into my booth and straightens the little hat on my head. "You have any questions, just push the intercom," he tells me while shutting the door. "I'll be close."

There are three movies showing tonight. A late afternoon matinee, followed by two evening shows. For the first, I chose to give people blue tickets. There's no rhyme or reason. Of the three colors, I just start with blue.

Not long after the movie starts, I discover just how dull my new job is. Everything is silent. Every minute lets itself be known. I had brought my Native American History books, but I don't quite feel right working through them. At least not with this being my first day. Even though I'm in a tiny booth at the theater entrance where nobody can really see me, I still feel like I ought to be making a good first impression. So instead of doing homework I just sit, watching nothing exciting happen out the window. An occasional car passes. Some old folks walk by. I give them a little smile and they return the gesture. After an hour or so a group of kids ride by on bikes. They don't seem to notice me.

Within an hour I'm slouching. The ache beneath my shoulders gets me thinking about how crooked my back will be when I'm an old lady. I watch the final moments of daylight slip away from behind some buildings on the far side of the street. The buildings themselves don't offer much entertainment themselves. Directly across from the theater is a law firm. Next to it, a dentist's office. Three buildings down was some family restaurant called The Pie Hole. I've never heard of it, but have no doubt I'll become acquainted with its menu at some point or another. It starts to dawn on me that, honestly, this is most peaceful I've felt in a long time. I'm bored, but it's been several hours and I haven't stressed about money. I haven't been feeling anxious over this second shot with Wyanet. I'm just here. In a new place. Working. Bored and in need of something with back support, but this isn't half bad.

For the next show I decide on yellow tickets.

About twenty minutes after the movie starts, I twist my way out of the booth and crutch a few quick laps around the lobby. When I return to my post, the world is quiet again. It's dark enough outside that I can kind of see my reflection in the window, and I make note of how stupid the little hat looks on my head. I look down at my backpack wedged into the corner and start to contemplate my homework.

That's when he steps back into my life.

How I miss him coming is beyond me. The man's as big as an outhouse and has the subtlety of a car horn. But he practically appears out of nowhere and asks, "You folks e'er play that one 'bout the talking pig?"

I look up, (and up and up) and meet Gus's eyes. He stands on the other side of the booth, looking back down at me. His one eye is still bloodshot, and as he scratches his beard a couple random flakes of God knows what fall out.

"You know," he says, "fuckin' pig and all them animals talk. Then there's these sheep n' shit at the end."

"I- I don't think so," I tell him. "What are you doing here?"

He shrugs, lifting one hand. He's holding a Styrofoam cup with a straw. For some reason I find the lack of a lid unsettling. He sucks on the straw a moment and then spits the contents on the ground. I can't quite tell what it is through the glass, but its brown. "Jus' paintin' the town red, I s'pose," he says, a fat smirk across his face. Then, "So you showin' that pig movie er what? Love that movie." He chuckles. "*That'll do pig*," he says, more to himself than me I think.

I lean into the glass and say, “You don’t even remember me, do you?”

“Sure do,” he tells me. “Yer that frigid bitch from the other night. Still got my knife?”

“What?”

“Oh uh,” he slurps from his drink again and spits it onto the ground. The bite marks on the end of the straw glisten.

“Stop spitting!” I snap. “That’s disgusting!”

He laughs. “Ya’ll got no idea. But really, if ye still got m’knife, I’d like to have ‘er back. Seminal reasons. Was the one ya got stabbed in yer leg.”

I think he meant *sentimental* but feel no need to correct him. Instead I say, “No, I don’t have your knife! I was unconscious at the hospital when they removed it. It’s probably been confiscated by the police. Maybe you should take it up with them.”

“Oh yeah?” He shrugs. “And you ain’t playin’ the movie with the talkin’ pig?”

“Are you for real?” I ask.

He looks down at me with a blank expression.

I say, “No. We’re not playing the stupid pig movie.”

“Well you oughta,” he says. “My favorite. Ya’ll start playin’ it, I’ll buy a ticket every showin.’ Where’s the law in this town anyways?”

“Are you on drugs or something?”

“Kinda drunk,” he shrugs. Then he rolls his head back and breathes in the air. Like he’s sniffing for something. “Still got some time,” he utters. Then he asks, “So where’m I s’posedta get m’knife back? Where’s the law around here?”

I stare up at him and he just looks blankly down at me. A few random things to be said cross my mind but, ultimately, I decide they’re not even worth it. So I point in the general direction of the police station. He stares me down a moment longer and says, “*That’ll do pig*.” Then he takes a few steps back, shakes his Styrofoam cup, and tosses it over his shoulder.

“Hey!” I scream, but he ignores me and starts walking down the street, evidently toward the police station.

When his cup hits the ground, it lands in the middle of the road, directly under the light of a lamp. A thick brown mess spatters out of it. It looks like either barbeque sauce or diarrhea. I wouldn't be surprised if he'd been drinking either.

Eventually people start lining up for the late show. At this point I notice how the earliest show was made up mostly of elderly people and families, while the middle show was a more varied crowd. This audience is almost entirely college students. As a very welcome surprise, Kyla and Candace are some of the first in line.

"Oh, God!" Kyla laughs. She snaps a few pictures of me with her phone. "I love the hat, F-Bomb. Just. Love it! You have to wear that all the time."

Candace, equally delighted, is a bit more gentle. She asks, "How's your first night going?"

"Not bad," I say. I try to be quick with conversation, exchanging money for red movie tickets. "I saw that guy again. The one from the bar with the machete."

"Oh my God!" Kyla says. "Are you serious? Did you talk to him?"

"He kept asking if we're showing a movie about a pig and wanted his knife back," I tell them as I slide their tickets under the window. "I'll tell you about it tonight," I say, realizing I basically told them the entire story already.

"Okay," Candace says. "Oh, Joanie said she's sorry she can't make it, but we should call her after the movie. We can all go to Waldo's or something."

I sell tickets to another dozen people or so, and the next person in line is Wyanet. I can feel how hard I'm grinning as I say, "You came?"

She smiles. "I've just decided you look really cute in hats."

I blush. I can't see myself all that well in the reflection, but my face definitely just turned the same bright shade of red as the tickets I'm selling. I smirk. I love the way her golden eyes are so vibrant against her black hair. As I lean forward, sliding her ticket through, the reflection of my eyes lines up with her face. I don't really know what to say about it. For a quiet second, I just let myself feel in awe that she's here and I get to appreciate her. Of course, I'm still on my first night of the job, so I don't let myself linger for too long.

Maybe. Time is a bit fuzzy at the moment. "Did you see Candace and Kyla are here?" I ask. "They want to hang out after I'm done."

Wyanet nods. "I saw them go inside while I was getting in line. I was going to join them but the guy behind them was being a dick about me cutting, so I left. But yeah, they're saving me a seat."

Our fingers graze when she takes her ticket. "You know it's the same movie we saw the other night," I say.

"Maybe I'll pay attention this time," she shrugs. "I'll see you after."

Another dozen people and another dozen tickets go by. As it gets closer to showtime, the line dies off and eventually disappears. I'm allowed to leave the booth after the final showing has been playing for an hour, so at this point I'm just counting down the minutes. Soon I'll be doing whatever cleaning duties I can from my crutches. After the movie, I'll join my friends. Not bad for a first night on the job. For a moment I think of glancing at my homework, but decide there's no sense in starting it here when I'll just be packing it back up soon anyway.

Instead, I watch life go by outside the window.

There's the Legal firm.

The Pie Hole.

The brown stain and discarded cup under a street lamp. Now with some guy sprawled out over it.

There's the dentist's office.

Wait.

I adjust my glasses. Where did he come from? Right below the street lamp, he's stretched out on his fingers and toes, his face directly over the stain. He wears an a white leisure jacket over a gleaming red shirt. His black tie drags on the cement, but he doesn't seem to care. He's poised over the stain from Gus's drink, cocking and twisting his head. He sniffs it like a dog. And then, ever so slowly, he lowers his head. I can just barely make out his tongue lapping a little taste.

He hisses and spits, leaping to his feet. Even then, he can't seem to take his eyes off the spill. He paces around it, studying it from every angle, a small scowl on his pale face.

After several minutes of watching him, I sit back and my stool creaks.

He snaps his head toward me. He watches me, and although his eyes are covered in shadow, they have the faint glimmer to them. It must be from the marquee lights.

He relaxes his shoulders and grins. He struts towards me, going through the motion of smoothing his hair with his fingers. His hair isn't even long. The cut screams military to me; shaved on the sides with some length on top. Enough for him to be able to flick his hair to the side with a shake of his head. Which he does. Twice.

"Hey there," he says. His voice smooth and certain. He slides one hand into his pocket while swinging the other to his step. Several gold chains dangle at his waist. They match the gaudy ruby encrusted rings on his fingers. He keeps his face at a deliberate downward angle, though he keeps his eyes trained on me. His each and every move is so deliberate that I wonder how often he rehearses. If he breaks into a dance or a flash mob forms behind him, I wouldn't be surprised. "I didn't see you there," he says once he's reached the booth window. He leans down a little, looking into my eyes. The letters *YOLO* are tattooed in his neck. Both *O*'s encircle little scars. He says, "and you didn't see me either."

It's the strangest thing; I'm overwhelmed with the feeling that he's right. I didn't see him. I still don't see him. He's right here, right in front of me. But I must be mistaken because, just like he told me, I know I can't possibly be seeing him. In the back of my mind, I feel little sparks of anxiety. The fact that I can see him and not see him at the same time makes me want to hyperventilate. But I don't move. I breathe softly. I have no rational objection to him standing there, even though he is...n't. I even tell him, "I don't see you. How could I? You're not here."

"Good girl," he says, flicking his hair to the side again. "Now, you're going to forget me as soon as I leave, but-" he cuts himself off to look one way, then the other, "but prior to that, why don't you tell me how long that beautiful, *beautiful* bliss has been spilt, drying in the street over there."

"Two hours and twenty-seven minutes," I say, having never been more certain of time in my life. "Some chauvinist threw it there."

"Chauvinist?" he smiles. He looks into my eyes again, like he's studying me. "Tell me, do you prefer Emmeline, Millie, F-Bomb, or... Pie-Pie?"

Pie-Pie?

That's what my dad used to call me as a little girl. I hadn't thought of that name in years. *How did he know that?* I don't have it myself to ask him. I don't have anything in myself but a profound need to answer his question. "Millie," I tell him. "But nobody ever calls me Millie. They always call me F-Bomb. It's because of this one time I cursed. I got a B-on a really great paper about the flora in and on our bodies." In the back of my mind I'm telling myself to stop talking.

"Millie," he says. "Good." He repeats my name a few times, grinning wider every time. His teeth are flawless, perfectly white. Even his gums are amazing, which I imagine is difficult with those enormous fangs. Flossing around those must be awful. But how does he have fangs? He's not even here. "Do you know what that is out there?"

"I don't. I honestly have no idea."

"Of course not," his smile is overwhelming. "How could you? I'll tell you," he says, grazing a finger along the bottom ledge of the window, "I've been smelling it for days now. It's all over this godforsaken town, lingering in the air like some sweet and unattainable dream. Oh, but not like this. This is different. Before it's been in a tiny drop or dry stain. Nothing like this," he dramatically waves his hand toward the glob in the street and snaps, "I thought there was a real feast in the road for a moment!" He cackles. There's something entirely inconsistent about him. I suppose that's bound to happen when someone isn't really here. "And now I can't even taste it without it making me ill."

He presses his forehead against the window and sighs. His bangs smoosh against the glass. He looks me over, the way men always do. But instead of lingering on my chest, he sniffs. "Millie?" his smile grows wider. Too wide for a person. "Oh, my darling Millie. You've been injured." His nostrils flare. He twists his head, sniffing through the opening at the base of the window.

I can't take my eyes away from him, which is so strange. He told me he wasn't here. I'm so sure of it. He isn't here at all. "I was stabbed," I tell him. "Some guy dropped a machete on me. Not the same one who made a mess in the street. But it's his fault."

He sniffs harder, pushing his nose as far into the opening as he can. When he finally exhales, it comes out as long, low groan. If he was actually here, I'd swear he just had an orgasm. "Oh, Millie," he says, "Millie, Millie, Millie. I understand you now. What a lovely, *lovely* girl you are."

In a heartbeat, shattered glass is dicing my face. I'm certain he's gone. He was never here. But he's closer than ever. He's through the window, licking his fangs with a forked tongue. His hands are ringing my throat. He's not here, but he's yanking me out of my booth. He's dragging me down the sidewalk. He's saying, "Let's go for a walk."

We zip down several blocks in an instant. My hat flies off in the process. We're moving too fast for me to see where it went. My stupid, *stupid* little hat. My first paycheck is going to be short twenty dollars.

Why couldn't it have been the bowtie?

And how are my glasses staying on?

My body jounces along the sidewalk. He has me by the hand, jostling me like a ragdoll against a belt sander. My legs flop and dance, leaving a drizzled, bread crumb trail of blood along our path. I want to fight; to writhe off the pain of my calves grinding down to their bones. But there's nothing in me. For all the agony, as houses whip by in a blur, I have no control of myself. This must be what dying is like. Deep within, I'm floating along, experiencing raw pain, feeling too distant to react. Like it's all a dream. Not the kind I can awaken from. But I'm sure I could distance myself if my soul would just gnaw off the umbilical cord attached to all this suffering.

I try to scream, but only manage to drool a few noiseless bubbles.

"Oh-ho! You *are* a feisty one," he cackles. "It's been so long since we've had a good sacrifice."

Two seconds and three blocks later he rambles on, "Such a thing-such a *sweet* young thing. A virgin in your condition. Unspoiled. The one who offered you? He must be strong-willed." I don't understand. I'm not a virgin.

He rounds a corner. I swing and he pulls me against the centrifugal force, dislocating my shoulder. I manage another pitiful bubble. He keeps running, saying, "Of course I appreciate his mystique. It was a man you said, wasn't it? The one who stabbed you. Oh, no matter. I'll meet him soon enough!"

He slows at the gate of a two-story house with charcoal, gray siding and a black awning over the porch. He drags me over a patchy lawn. It's littered with pocked mounds of dirt. It's like giant ant hills. From a few of the holes, I see the gleam of beady eyes. Something darts by us. A little blur. Must be a rat. I must be hallucinating because I swear it has a cape.

We reach the porch. My captor drops me at his side and some of my wounds spurt at the impact. He fiddles through his pockets, producing a ring of about a dozen keys. He rattles his way through them. His eyes are wild as he fidgets for the right one. Between smirks and grimaces, he garbles a blend of snarls, grunts, and groans. He licks his fangs and bites his lip. He's speaking quietly, mumbling to himself in either another language or just random syllables. He singles out one key and, after a few frantic attempts at the lock, he opens the door. I'm thrown inside.

The floor is wood and doesn't feel much better than the sidewalk. I want to turn my head, figure out where I am. Maybe even plan an escape route. But I still have no control. Even if I did, how much fight could I possibly have? How good is pure adrenaline when you're the epitome of road rash, have an inability to walk, and have a dislocated shoulder? Whatever defensive strategy I can form, it'll have to revolve around bleeding.

The door creaks shut. At first is seems to shut on its own. At least until I see, or at least think I see, another small blur. Another cape. I can't turn my head enough to look directly at it.

"My brood! My loves!" my captor sings out. "We have a guest!" He kicks me so I flop onto my other side. I'm facing a red suede chair, dimly lit by a lamp on a side table.

It's the only light in the room. I'm unable to make out anything beyond the chair.

"Please," my captor calls, "this mustn't wait!"

"Pipe down, Charles," a young woman's voice says from nearby. Her tone is somewhere between bored and mildly irked.

"Forgive me, Lianna," my captor, Charles I guess, says more softly. "It seems we're no longer the only night walkers in town. Look, look! Our new neighbor has graced us with a gift."

From the shadows beyond the chair, a pair of combat boots float into the light. They clop onto the floor, joined by two endless rivers of fishnets, flowing up porcelain white legs, into an abyss of black leather. As she steps forward, a magenta cape drapes around her pearlescent arms. "This was given to us?" She asks through glossy black lips. Her hair is shorter than Charles',buzzed down to a military length. Looking down at me, she says, "Did this neighbor feel a rat's carcass was insufficiently offensive?" A handful of silver studs, bars, and loops run through her ears, nose, and eyebrow, matching the collar around her neck and bracelets adorning her wrists. Her is skin milky and doll-like, complimenting her attire like yin and yang. If I'd seen her under other circumstances-if I wasn't unresponsive or bleeding all over the floor-I'd probably chicken out from calling her gorgeous. "I know this smell," she whispers. Her eyes thin as she studies me. Her expression isn't unlike how I'd judge a food wrapper on the ground, several feet from a trash bin. To Charles she asks, "You found her like this? Is the bowtie meant to be ironic?"

Charles shrugs. "Apologies, sister. I found her quite fresh. Only a wound through her thigh. In my excitement I dragged her here. My speed was perhaps too aggressive on the girl." Then louder, with ringmaster bravado he calls out, "But where, Dear Sister, are Levy and Ellis? How are they not here already?"

"I am here," a low voice grunts from another shadow. A curtain to the side of the room opens, revealing a small reading nook, lit only by moonlight. A silhouette of a man- a *beast* made entirely of muscle, sits within, holding a hardcover book. His chiseled edges catch moonbeams. I don't know if this is the blood loss speaking, but his biceps are the size of me.

"Leviathan!" Charles smiles. "Look upon this feast!"

Leviathan looks my way. Darkness hides his features, but his eyes hold a catlike shine. He draws the curtain shut and approaches, into the light. His hair is sandy, spiked straight up. His beard is a pointed, devilish strap. As he leans over me, his face lights up the way a child does at the sight of a puppy. "Oooh, a young lady," he swoons. "Such an exquisite flower, Brother." As he kneels, I hear the stitches strain in his cowboy boots and low-cut jeans. He also wears hunter green tank top that will most assuredly rip the moment he flexes anything. He studies me fondly, raising one eyebrow. "Such a nimble, little waif, isn't she? Oh, but that *smell.* You say she was left for us? Who could cast aside such a virgin goddess?"

"A chauvinist, I'm told."

Levy gasps. "A sucking bastard!" I can't tell if he's being sarcastic or genuinely aghast.

Charles chuckles. He walks around me with a hop in his step. He continues to lick his lips and smile. "The girl knows nothing. Not even that she's an offering. But please. Where is Father? Where is Ellis?"

An old man's voice comes from somewhere, everywhere in the room. "I am here, Charles," he says. "We've all been waiting here. You left in such a hurry, we thought perhaps something was the matter."

Leviathan and Lianna step back toward the chair. They cross paths, and as they move to either side, a formally dressed man is suddenly occupying the seat. It's as though he's been sitting there all along. I just couldn't see him until this moment. He appears older, perhaps in his fifties or sixties, except for what appears to be a tribal tattoo on his temple, extending back into his silver, haystack hair. He wears a gray pin-striped suit with a maroon shirt. His tie is black, tacked by a diamond that sparkles in the lamp light. He sits with his legs crossed, an open book dangling from his hand. Leviathan and Lianna stand at either side of him, posed as if to accentuate their apparent father between them.

I don't see any resemblance. At least not until Ellis smirks at me, revealing fangs twice the length of Charles'. He sets his book on the side table and leans in. He looks to

Charles as if to say something but waves him off and gives me a grin. He says, “Are you frightened, Little Darling?”

“Yes,” I say. My voice is flat, incapable of inflection. The words are true but automatic. Like I'm speaking reflexively. “I am frightened and confused.”

“As you should be,” he says. “You see, we are-”

“Vampires,” I interrupt him. Consciously, I'm screaming, wrestling with the fangs, the dark room, and all the pain searing through my broken bloodied body. Yet I can't help but speak to him passively, still in a dream-state. Or back on those wonderful hospital drugs. God, I could use those drugs right now. “I see you're supposed to be vampires. But is this is real or some staged façade? Are you real vampires or just kidnappers? Is this a fetish game? Are you going to rape me?”

Ellis sighs. “I was going to say we're *children of the night*.”

Leviathan slaps a hand over his heart, “My Flower, I would-I could never perform such an unconscionable act!”

Lianna chimes in, “No. But you'll certainly drain of her blood, chop her to bits, and burn the pieces in the cellar. Save for a lock of hair for your beloved scrapbook.”

Leviathan adds, “And scatter her ashes in the garden, of course. To become a part of the flowers. Ashes to ashes and dust to dust. Beauty grows from the carnage of our survival. Rest assured I'd never, ever allow myself to forget her.”

“Who was that freckled red-head from June, three years ago. The one with the curls?”

Leviathan lowers his gaze. He stares off into nothing. “Marriette?”

“Marriette was a black girl who'd lost her parents. Kelly was the red-head. Kelly Nemzek. She was your human brother's descendent. And you made it weird.”

Leviathan hisses, scowling at Lianna.

“Whatever,” Lianna shrugs. “You're the one who told her she had eyes like your mother.”

Ellis lifts a hand, “Children, children. Please, you're scaring our guest.” He never takes his eyes off of me. Not even when he lifts himself from the chair and floats toward me. “Nosferatu, you might call us. The walking dead. Yes, my darling. We are cursed, damned to feed upon the living and never again behold the sun. We are, each of us, vampires. And you, I must regretfully say, have been offered to us as a feast." He lands beside me and kneels. "But you do not fear death," he tells me.

"I do not fear death," I tell him, and very suddenly I've never been so convinced of anything before in my life. I don't know if he meant for this, but in the back of my mind, I feel myself enraged. I am not afraid of death, but I want to stake his heart for killing me.

"You pity us for the creatures we've become," he says, "and admire us for how much greater we must seem."

"I pity and admire you," I tell him.

And I do. I truly do. But that doesn't mean I can't hate him.

"And you wish to be our sacrifice," he says, grazing a finger along my machete wound. It stings, but I barely have it in me to twitch my leg. As he says the words, I can't agree more. I do want to be his sacrifice. It's the only way I'll get him to choke on my blood.

That'll do pig.

The words echo in the back of my thoughts. Another voice. Somewhere. The faintest echo.

That'll do pig.

All the pain, pity, and admiration are gone. I only feel the anger. I only feel absolute hate for the vampire standing over me. He lifts his finger. A drop of my blood clings to his fingernail. Somewhere deep within, a part of me thinks I can destroy him with it.

That'll do pig.

Louder.

He hovers over me, a crooked grin on his face as he brings his bloodied finger to his lips. "You were passive in life, weren't you? Sweet and innocent." He licks my blood off his finger and his smile vanishes. "Charles!" he snaps, standing upright in an instant. I hadn't even seen him move.

"Father?" I hear Charles say, but can't see from where. Somewhere behind me.

"Her blood," Ellis says. "This child is bleeding from every pore," he says. "Her blood tastes thin. It is low. Look! Look at the floor behind her! You left streaks of her blood all over my floor. Didn't you carry her? Tell me you didn't drag her the entire way!"

"Ellis," Charles says. "I did not think-"

"This I see," Ellis snaps. He waves his hands over me. "This is a virgin. An adult virgin! You do not drag her through the streets like a common whore. You left half of her blood outside, haven't you? We can't drink her in this state. A feast as rich as her should be preserved. Drained over weeks and allowed to replenish. In this state I doubt we'll get a night from her."

"Forgive me," Charles says. I hear a thud behind me and his voice seems closer. I think he dropped to his knees. From how they're speaking, I wouldn't be surprised if he buried his face in his hands and wept. The pansy faggot.

That'll do pig.

Wait. What did I just think? I don't talk like that. Was that Charles? Ellis? How many minds do I have in here?

That'll do pig.

That wasn't me.

Ellis is screaming at Charles, circling me. "Why would you bring *this* into our home? A snack? A tease of a meal meant for a feast? You've spoiled your dinner, Child! To drink her now would be a waste!"

"Forgive me," Charles whines, "forgive me. How might I set this right? Perhaps I could chain her in the cellar and nurse her until she's refilled?"

"Chain her in the-?" Ellis stands and screams, "Really? Really?" He moves over me in a dash. An instant later, Charles is thrown over my head, skidding against the floor until he collides into the wall. Levy cowers. A little smirk curls on Lianna's black lips. "We are not monsters, Charles! We are *vampires*! Have you no dignity for your kind?" He floats over me, his hands outstretched, fingers poised like claws for some reason.

I can't help but recall my mother. When I was ten, when dad was deployed, she took me to see *Cats*. We would do the same thing with our hands, joking. But this is real. Ellis is middle aged man. Fingers splayed like cat claws. For real.

Charles uses the wall to stand. "I'm sorry, father," he says, "forgive me."

With a grumble, Ellis relaxes his fingers. So much for the ferocity of Andrew Lloyd Webber. "There is no apology for youth and stupidity." He floats back to the floor. "You must be given a responsibility." Ellis waves a hand and the furniture glides away to the furthest wall. A little flick of the wrist and Charles is thrown to the ground beside me. He lifts his head and hisses, his fangs only inches from my face. Ellis's tone changes; he sounds statesman-like. "Make this child your ghoul."

Charles shuts his mouth. After several nostril flaring breaths his lower lip begins to tremble. Red tears well in his eyes. He looks afraid. "Father?" he whimpers. How is he the same vampire who yanked me through a window? "Why?" he asks.

"Did I tell you to question me?" Ellis points down at Charles, slowly twirling his finger. Charles tenses. His head shakes like he's fighting against something pushing down on him. "You will make this virgin your ghoul. You will bind your soul to hers, dress her wounds, heal her body, and see to her every need. You will love her. And when that day comes when the two of you can never part, the rest of us will slaughter her before you. We will savor every drop of her essence. We will mutilate her body. And *you will endure it*." Charles raises his head. He opens his mouth to speak but words seem lost on him. Ellis continues to rant. "You will not drink of her. You've already wasted more than your share. You dragged a carefully prepared sacrifice like a sack of potatoes. Just think if the Guardians had tasted her. We'd never get the shreds off the lawn."

I think back to all the mounds and holes in the front yard. There had been eyes. Glimmering eyes, like Leviathan's. Cats? Do they have a bunch of cats out there?

I snap out of the pondering when Lianna and Leviathan step forward. Lianna says, "To give Charles a ghoul, father? Surely there is some other punishment. When we feast on her, he will feel every bite. It'll be as though his own life is being ripped from him."

"That's the point, Dear Daughter," Ellis says. He stares down Charles and me, unmoving, unblinking. "Another vampire has come to our city. An old one, I'd wager, preparing such a neighborly gift for us. Perhaps Charles is too naïve to understand, but to not feed on a pure virgin himself delivers a message. He acknowledges our territory. He says he won't indulge on the best of our livestock. He took the time to seek out, bleed, and offer us a banquet. To tear through such a gift shows indignity. If this vampire saw Charles dragging her along, we've wasted the time and courtesy extended to us. I will not insult a guest. We must show acceptance. The only means of which, the only option Charles leaves us with, is redemption. He ruined a gift. He will restore it with time and care. He will suffer for his disgrace."

"Let me," Leviathan chimes in. "I will take his punishment."

Confusion drifts into Charles' expression. He, Ellis, and Lianna all face Leviathan. Even I can't help but feel a bit caught up in the twist. Whatever is going on, I must admit, it's more entertaining than sitting inside a ticket booth. Not that I have much choice. I can't control my body. My mind is adrift, separate from myself. Not drugged, but like there's a barrier between me and the world. Like I can see it all happening but I am somehow blocked from it. Confined to my own space and only a witness to the vampire's melodrama. It's like I'm watching it all… from, well, from inside a ticket booth.

Leviathan lifts a hand. "Hear me out," he says, then pauses as if expecting some objection. When none comes, he continues. "Look at her. Helpless, broken, and bleeding to death on our floor. Have you ever seen a creature so pure? Has there ever been a sight more pitiful than the candle of her life struggling against its extinguishment? I think… I know… I love her."

Ellis rubs his own temples.

Leviathan saunters around me. He extends a hand as if I should grab hold of him. "I can think of no better way to honor our gift than to than to make her my own. I will nurse every wound, cleaning them with my tongue if I must. I will cherish her every breath every thundering heartbeat until her last. When the time comes to snuff her life, when she's finally well enough to endure her destiny as our sacrifice, I will taste her blood. I will feel her soul fade from within my own." He drops to one knee, ascending his hand into the air. "I will carry the sorrow of her passing for all eternity. She may die, but our love...our love will truly be the stuff of immortality."

I half expect a short round of applause, but instead Ellis kicks Leviathan into the wall. "I told you to quit reading those fucking books!" he screams.

Lianna utters, "Stuff of immortality?" with a small giggle.

Ellis grabs Charles by the nape of his neck. "Now!" he screams, practically rubbing his nose at my breast.

Charles doesn't argue. His breath is heavy. Every exhales stings the scrapes and gashes along my side. I can't flinch it away. The pain itself is distant from whatever spell my mind is under. I feel it, but any reaction I might have is banging on the window, begging to be let in. I wonder if this what death is supposed to feel like. Drifting somewhere both deep within and outside of myself. Acutely aware of my body's agony, but feeling it separate from own experience. My body is some horrible, mangled thing I should be done with. Why would I want to be alive? Am I still alive? How? And seriously, how are my glasses still on?

"She's slipping," Ellis says. "Hurry. Not the throat. She's lost too much already. Just take a little. Enough to bind. But do not turn her."

Charles hesitates. *The pussy.* He lifts me into his arms; cradles me. He looks me in the eyes and says, "I'm sorry. But you will forgive me. You will love me for this."

I say, "I forgive you. I love you."

I can still talk?

That'll do pig.

His fingers dig into my back. He pulls me tight against him. He hisses, then bites into my shoulder. However distant my pain was before, it all rubber bands back. This hurts. Paralyzing, agonizing pain on top of pain on top of pain. Every part of me he doesn't have in his grasp convulses. He grabs me tighter. His fingernails stab. Pins and needles numb my fingers and toes, then hands and feet. Arms and legs are next. The agony doesn't leave me, but swells into my shoulder. It empties from my limbs and fills my center like toothpaste in rolled up tube. And Charles is lapping it up. Not just my blood, but gushes and globs of suffering. He laps up my agony, and his tongue tickles my shoulder while he's at it.

In the few vampire stories I read as a girl, they never mentioned the tongue tickling. They don't say how it feels like a mad dog biting into you while playfully licking your skin at the same time. Not to mention his little groans of delight between swallows. As he drinks, something creeps up against my back. Something jabs. *Dear God, this is getting him hard.*

"That's enough," Ellis says.

Charles doesn't show any signs of slowing down.

"You've had your only taste, Boy," Ellis warns. "Savor the memory. Release her. Give back all you've taken."

Charles continues to lick, groan, and moan. His fingernails dig deeper into my back and he starts to shimmy, grinding my hip against the crotch of his pants.

"Enough!" Ellis screams.

Charles is ripped from me. I flop back onto the floor. At least I think it's the floor. It feels more like a void. The separation- no, the distance is back. More so than before. Everything is dark. There's screaming, but the words are so far. I can barely make it out.

"Father, I can't!"

"Do it!"

Something-something, "-drain her!"

"Be a-," something or other.

Everything is soft.

Everything is silent.

That'll do pig.

The thing about feeling time stop is that it's the opposite of going numb. Time doesn't grind to a halt. It's more like your inability to feel the past and future seeps away. Your life doesn't just flash before your eyes. You're in every moment, all at once. Gradually at first. Like… imagine pouring a bottle of eggnog onto the floor. Thick, creamy eggnog. You watch the puddle grow, shape, and curve. You can touch any single point in the puddle when you're focused. But when time slips away, you lose your focus, and realize you're touching every point of the puddle all at once. Because the puddle is you.

More interesting is the sensation of the gap. A hole within your presence of time. The world, the people you love, the things you're used to, and all the new surprises around every corner; it's all still there. Every part of it. But there's this dry spot puddle curves around. You can't feel any of them, not because all those things are gone, but because you don't exist.

So later, *now* in a way, when I eventually experience time stop, I don't look back… It's not looking back. More like a curvature. I come out to Dad, as I watch Wyanet eat celery, as I fire a gun outside a karaoke club, as I watch a missile take orbit, as I introduce myself to Joanie, as I teethe, as I have all my orgasms, as I watch Gus rip a head off a dog, as I contemplate suicide, as I charge into Armageddon, as I read all my books, as I adjust the socks Mom made me for Hanukkah. I'm in all of these moments, but not here. I'm not in this dry spot.

So...where am I?

So, if asked what being dead feels like, the most accurate way I can describe it is, *no longer being eggnog.*

I jolt.

I'm drinking… rust? Is rust a flavor?

The world returns. My eyes are dry. I feel like I've been micro-napping. Where I am, when I am, haven't changed. Or, only slightly changed.

I'm back in Charles's lap. *That's new*. I'm clutching his forearm in both hands, sucking blood out of his wrist. *Definitely new.* I try to jerk myself away but my fingers twinge then lock back down. I'll regard that as only somewhat new.

He smiles that stupid, fanged smile. Looking to Ellis, he says, "I feel her."

His gaze drifts down to me. When I look into his eyes, they appear gold. Then everything hazes over. Suddenly, I'm watching myself drink from his arm, through his eyes. Not just reflected in his pupils but I'm literally in his mind.

I'm...sad. I'm trying to ignore... elation? I feel a heart beating again. My heart. Not his. But I feel his heartbeat too. The pain in his wrist. A throb between his legs bobs to flaccidity as he remembers how jubilant he'd been to become a vampire twenty years ago. How desperately he'd wanted the dark gift. Now he feels this connection between us. Its palpable. Like energy. He wonders if I feel it too, and thinks to ask Ellis.

Charles looks away and the sensation is gone. Suddenly I'm back in the room, drinking his blood.

What just happened?

"That's enough," Ellis says. "I feel her soul, Charles. You've changed her. But not enough. She won't turn."

Charles lays me down. He wipes a bloody tear from his cheek and calls me a, "Good girl."

Four vampires stand over me like I'm an especially unique piece of roadkill. Leviathan puts a hand on Charles's shoulder. He's crying too.

Somewhere outside, out in the world, a man is yelling, "Wooooo!"

The ceiling explodes.

Lianna hisses. Leviathan shoves Charles behind him, fingers poised like cat claws as we're engulfed in a plume of dust and debris.

Charles scoops me up in one hand. He drags me to the corner farthest from the blast. My arm drags over something so I grab it. A piece of shattered house. I don't know if it's Charles making me clutch a weapon or something my body does on impulse. But now I have a piece of wood.

Across the room, dust billows away from the debris. Buried in a heap of planks and roof tiles, a thick, hairy arm twitches, then flops dead into the mess. As the air clears, I make out a bald head, mud colored beard, and two enormous eyes; one of them bloodshot. I know him! It's that chauvinist, lying dead in the mess. He must've fallen through the roof and landed in here.

Because that makes sense.

His eyes stare blankly in my direction. There's nothing in them. Whatever it was that made them a person is gone. He doesn't blink. He doesn't breathe. He's just a body.

"What the suck just happened?" Leviathan says, the ferocity of his cat-hands relaxing.

Ellis floats closer to the mess. He rolls in the air to look up at the new hole in his ceiling. "Quiet. And if you never say *what the suck* again, the world only stands to benefit."

I continue to watch Gus's eyes. They're empty. Dead. He's dead. Some puzzle pieces start shifting in my mind. Gus left that goop in the street. Charles found me because of him. But now he's dead. The vampires discussed me as a gift from another vampire. But now he's dead. Who was he? Why did he do all of this? Just to die?

-There's a little flicker in Gus's eye. Something faint. I'm not sure calling it a flicker is even right. It's just something. It takes me away from the floor of the vampires' house. Suddenly, a tiny neighborhood is beneath me. I'm in the sky. There's a trail of blood along the sidewalk, leading to a two story house with horrible lawn. I smell death below, and it makes me smile. The house starts getting bigger and bigger and-

Gus blinks.

What? I see myself, but from across the room. The wounds on my body healed. My scent is different. I smell like blood and mothballs. There's blood all around my mouth and holes in my shoulder. A word echoes in my thoughts, but not in my voice. It's his. It's Gus's. *Ghoul-*

He blinks again. *Dumb fuckers made 'er a ghoul.*

He looks away and suddenly I'm seeing him, back from across the room. His arm lifts then punches into the debris. Wood cracks. Dust plumes. He pushes some house off himself and worms out of the heap. "Did ya'll see that?" he coughs. He wobbles to his knees to the tune of popping joints and snapping bones. "Woo!"

"Cursed vampire!" Ellis screams. He grabs Gus by the collar with one hand and lifts him over his head. The action is probably meant to hold Gus in the air, but he stands easily and looks down at the old man throttling him. Somehow this doesn't give Ellis pause. "You've destroyed my house," he screams.

"Yeah," Gus chuckles, then leans forward and headbutts Ellis square on the nose.

Blood spurts as Ellis stumbles back. His nose is concave, flattened into his face. "You dare!" He screams, nasally.

Nearby, Leviathan says, "What the suck?" Again. I'm waiting for him to go full cat hands, but nothing happens. All the vampires are too stupefied to react.

Ellis pops his nose back. He licks blood off his philtrum. "You're not our kind," he says.

"Heh. Nope." Gus shrugs and then looks at me. Our eyes meet and I see myself sitting in the movie theater booth. For some reason my breasts are about five times larger, fighting against the buttons of my shirt. He looks away and I'm back in the room with him and four baffled vampires. "You turned her. One o' yall made 'er yer bitch," he says.

"Lowly *ghoul*!" Ellis screams. "Where is your master?"

"Wish I knew," he shrugs. "Pissy as ya'll faggot bitches are now, ain't nowhere near as furious as me at her."

The wood in my hand is rough, jagged. I graze its surface with my thumb, and it's a bit of a thrill. I'm using my thumb. All on my own! Vampires turning me into a ghoul, whatever that means. Raining chauvinists are rising from the dead. And here I am, fascinated that I've got wood. I mean-whatever. It's a sharp chunk of wood, probably a shard of a support beam. I turn it in my hand, taking in its edges. I turn it in my hand. I'm controlling it. *My hand. My arm.* For the first time since the ticket booth, I can move for myself. I look over to Charles, who's fixated on the scene in front of him. He's bearing his fangs at Gus, growling . He's distracted. Lianna too. She's standing at the door, doing that cat hands thing vampires seem to enjoy. I squeeze the wooden shard. I size up Charles.

Ellis doesn't take kindly to Gus's indifference. He floats down and screams, "Insolent!" as he punches Gus in the gut. Gus hunches over and doubles back, stumbling through some debris. He hits the far wall and drops to one knee. Blood oozes from his mouth. The other three vampires cheer. I drag myself to my feet, but stay low. They're distracted. Everybody is distracted as Ellis lowers out of the air and starts pounding on Gus. He yells between punches, "Insolent whelp! Where is-"

Two thoughts enter my mind. *Get out! Run!* So of course when my unleash my battle cry it sounds like, "Re-ount!" Which probably isn't the flashiest thing to scream when lunging at the person who abducted you, but whatever. I'm done. I'm ***done***! I drive the wooden shard into Charles's side, just below the ribs. He springs away, twisting, flailing as he lands. I got him.

Everybody screams. From the corner of my eye I catch Gus's beaten, bloodied face. Of course he's grinning. Even with teeth protruding out the side of his beard like a yarn of popcorn on a tree, he has the smile of a child on Christmas morning.

If nothing else, the image is motivational. I need out.

Lianna is at the door, so I improvise my escape. I'm up, on my feet, running for the chair. It doesn't take much effort to grab it by the armrests and throw it straight ahead. I don't even break my stride. The chair shatters through the window. I have my opening.

Leviathan lunges, but Lianna is thrown into him. They both crumble to the side as I sprint past. Gus laughs from where Lianna had been standing, "Cheese it, girl!" I springboard off the rubble, through the window. I did it! I'm free! I'm making my escape! At least until my foot catches the window sill.

I fall face first onto a mound of dirt. Something twists. Something rips. I gasp, but can't pull in air. I try to stand, but everything is swirls. I stumble through another mound and collapse onto my back.

Stake. Why it dawns on me now, fighting for air in a pile of dirt, I don't know. But I stabbed a vampire with a wooden *stake*. Why did I call it a shard?

I wonder if he'll be okay.

The world takes its sweet time orienting itself to my dizziness. I practice drawing breaths. It doesn't go well. I ache everywhere, but as I shift I realize a lot of searing from the road rash is gone. I rub my arms and they feel oddly smooth.

The wounds themselves are gone. Everything is healed. The stitches are pulling in my leg, which merits inspection. This is easy because my pants are in ribbons from being dragged across town. The bandage that covered the wound is loose but stayed in the remains of my pant leg. The machete wound itself is exposed through all the tatters. It's too dark to make out details, but feeling along its ridge, the crust of scab flakes away. The wound itself feels old.

From inside the house, Leviathan snarls, "Suck you! Suck you!" Gus cackles and something smashes. Ellis is commanding, "Hold him! Hold him down!" Clatter and catastrophe continue. There's no better time to leave. I find my footing, look to the fence and- oh dear. Something is standing in front of me, watching me. It's furry and small. Standing on its hind legs, it wouldn't reach my knee. Its eyes gleam in the dark and as I look into them, I'm suddenly aware of a small debate going through its mind. I smell like *the blood of Stupid*. But it's faint. I might not be food. But I could be. Just in case, it's sizing me up, forming a plan. If it climbs my leg and gnaws through my belly, up under the ribs, it should have no trouble biting directly into my heart. That's where the best blood is. That's how it'd like to eat me.

It cocks its head to the side, still unsure.

A few small squeaks come from behind me. Another dozen sets of eyes are watching me with the same uncertainty. Those I look into all have similar debates running through their minds. I back toward the fence. Slowly. More and more eyes appear with every step. Soon the entire lawn gleams like a murderous little galaxy at my feet. By the time I reach the gate, there are so many shining eyes it's almost difficult to notice the darkness between them.

Then a light passes. Quickly. From right to left. I see their furry little bodies for just a second. They're rodents, I think. Not rats. Their faces are flat. I try to make out more detail, but just as soon as the light appeared, it's gone.

But it passes again. Right to left.

I can make out their shapes, but that can't be right. They look like-

The light passes. Right to left.

They're black-tail prairie dogs. That doesn't make any sense. I used to have a biology teacher who had one as a pet. He'd bring it to class, and I remember him specifically saying that those were in more Southern regions. But here they are. Hundreds of them, all on this little lawn, and all of them staring at me. All of them questioning how fat they'll get from drinking the blood in my heart.

The light passes right to left.

And for some reason most them are wearing red or black capes.

The light passes again.

One prairie dog, slightly larger than the others takes a step toward me. As the light passes, I catch sight of his white mohawk, which would be adorable under other circumstances. When our eyes meet, he's the first one not thinking about biting into my heart. Rather, he feels the best blood is lapped up from empty eye sockets. Preferably while I'm still alive. That way my breath will warm his tummy as he drinks from the hole in my face.

Present circumstances aside, I think I'm getting a handle on whatever this is when I make eye contact. I look into someone's, or evidently, something's eyes and I'm able to experience their thoughts. I don't want to say read. This isn't a conscious effort. I'm definitely not trying to make it happen. Now that I know black-tail prairie dogs enjoy warm dying breath on their tummy-tums, I can say with certainty I'd rather not know anybody's thoughts ever again. But in the compiling string of madness that is tonight, between the vampires, undead misogynists, and horde of murderous prairie dogs, I can at least say I have a grip on the fact that making eye contact results in terrible things.

The light passes again and it finally dawns on me that it's coming from somewhere. Specifically, above. I look up to spot a helicopter spinning out of control over the house. Because why wouldn't there be a helicopter? It drops, closer and closer, its searchlight whirring round and round.

I'd like to say I have the good sense to turn and run from such a thing. I'd love to be able to say that about myself. But instead I just scream and fall on my butt.

There's an explosion as the helicopter smashes into the roof. All the prairie dogs turn to the blast. Many of them bark and chirp under the roar of a mushroom cloud. The helicopter blades continue to spin, shredding the house from the inside. Flames and glass burst out of every window. Gus joins the calamity, bursting out the front door with someone's arm in his hand. He waves it like a trophy over his head, stepping on prairie dogs the entire way, not seeming to notice them. "Woo!" he screams again, stopping when he sees me. His teeth, somehow back on the inside of his cheek. Actually, where his teeth had been sticking out before, I don't even see any sign of a wound. "Oh good! Yer still here!" he laughs, lifting me to my feet. Our eyes meet. I see myself stabbing Charles. But the memory is off because it's as though I'm watching it happen from across the room, outside my own body. And my breasts are larger. But the image is gone as soon as Gus says, "What you done back there! I ain't never seen nobody do that! I didn't know nobody could do that!"

"Um, Gus," I whisper.

"Woo!" he screams again, flexing a muscle. "And you done did it! You killed that vampire that done made ya his ghoul!"

"Gus!" I say.

"High five?" He holds up the severed arm.

I point at the lawn.

He turns around. All the prairie dogs are looking at him. "Well that ain't good," he says flatly. Back in the rubble of the house, Lianna is smirking as blood trickles down her nose. Ellis steps up. His shirt is tattered, revealing jagged, spidery tattoos across his chest. Behind him, Leviathan approaches, one arm missing. There's about two hundred and fifty-three sets of eyes on us. Along with them, two hundred and fifty-three pairs of lips. All at once, they hiss. All the prairie dogs, every one of them, has two fangs on either side of their buck teeth.

Gus screams, "Cheese it!" and grabs me by the waist. He slings me over his shoulder, leaping over the gate. For the second time in less than an hour, I find myself being carried like a rag doll through the city streets. I'm bounced and jostled against Gus's shoulder, my belly repeatedly being thumped into his rock hard shoulder. It's difficult to breathe and the only thing keeping me steady is his hand pressing down on-

"Are you squeezing my butt?" I snap.

"Jus' didn't realize they came that boney!" He laughs and his hand moves slightly higher.

Every bit of anger building at him is dissipated by the sight of the horde chasing us. It's unreal. Even with everything else that's happened tonight, this is unreal. The vampire prairie dogs are fast, but seem to slow themselves down when in a group. Instead of all them chasing us on foot, they desperately clamber over one another, fangs bared, fighting to be the first to reach us. As a whole, they look like a wave of fur with little red and black capes. Some are quicker than others. The occasional prairie dog leaps off the crest of them, flinging itself forward. Somehow Gus is fast enough to stay ahead. The prairie dogs are consistently falling short behind us. But the wave of them keeps growing and growing as more prairie dogs join in. There could be hundreds- thousands more.

I don't see the other vampires for the first few blocks. Eventually I spot Lianna's face peek up above the prairie dog horde, then disappear behind it. "Out of the way!" she screams, but it doesn't seem to have an effect. "Go! Go!"

A moment later, the prairie dog wave breaks in an explosion of fur and capes. Little rodents fly in every direction as Ellis rushes ahead of them, flying several feet above the ground. He yells, "Return my son's arm!" as he stretches out both arms and opens his fingers, readying to clutch onto us.

"Fuck off!" Gus yells over his shoulder. Then to me, "Hang on, girl! We're nearly sumplace safe!"

I glance at Gus's free hand. Sure enough, he's still carrying Leviathan's arm. While I'm looking, something else catches my interest. Holstered at Gus's far side is a big, shiny revolver. I look up at Ellis closing in on us. His fingers widen. His jaw unhinges and his fangs elongate. I reach across Gus's back to grab hold of the gun. I miss and my fingers glides across the small of his back. It's sweaty.

"Thank me later, girl! No time fer foreplay!"

I ignore him. Ellis is flying closer. Closer. Behind him, Lianna is sprinting so fast that her legs are a blur. Behind her, the prairie dog wave has reformed and is somehow even larger than before. I try again for the gun. I manage to grab hold of his belt and tug myself toward the weapon.

Ellis is closing in.

I grab the gun and yank it from its holster. It's heavier than expected. Much heavier than anything my Dad let me fire as a kid. I nearly drop it, but manage to wrap my other hand around and thumb the hammer.

“Don’ you dare!” Gus screams. “Don’ you dare pull that trigger!”

Ellis widens his arms as he inches in on us.

Then it happens again. I see myself through Ellis. It’s like looking in a mirror. I’m being bounced around on Gus’s shoulder, his giant arm grasping me in place. I’m holding a gun, struggling to lift it. There are feelings in the reflection. Anger. Hatred. Confusion. I catch little flashes of myself stabbing Charles in the side. Ellis has a little daydream of chaining me down and beating me. For days. Even weeks. He rips open my neck and drinks out all of my blood, then spills his blood into my corpse. I awaken, heal, and he does it all over again.

That’s enough. I stiffen my arms. Through his gaze, I take aim until I can see straight down the barrel.

“Millie!” Gus screams.

I ignore him. I pull the trigger. Big mistake.

Ellis’s eye explodes in a red mist. The recoil of the gun bucks us both. Gus squeezes down on my back as the force of the shot throws us forward. I lose my grip on the revolver and everything is a blur. We hit ground, tumble, and slide forward. I catch a glimpse of the grass as I’m crunched against it. As I come to a stop, there’s a vampire prairie dog lunging for my face.

It gets squashed by a boot.

“Go!” Gus yells, “Into the church! I’ll hold ‘em off!” He grabs me by the arm and hoists me up like a twig. He shoves me. When I look ahead, we’re at the front entrance to a church. It’s familiar. I don’t know it’s name, but I’ve walked by it plenty of times in the past few years. We’re only about a few miles from my apartment. I stumble a few steps toward the church and a prairie dog flies over my shoulder. It crashes into the church doors and bursts. Like- spontaneously combusts upon impact. The church doors fling open. One of them slightly off its hinges. Where there had been a prairie dog, a small rain of ash scatters onto the floor.

That’s all I have to see. I run up the stairs three at a time, tripping over the top one, of course. I don’t fall, but battle for my balance until I’m safely in the building. I turn to shut the doors. Several more prairie dogs leap at me. I flinch. They reach the doorway and burst. Ashes waft at my face. A little gets up my nose. Okay, I think. That’s right. Vampires can't enter churches. There are far too many implications to go along with that thought, so instead I just try to fix the door, to seal myself inside. As soon as I grab the handle, the whole door breaks free off its hinges. As if anything tonight would go right.

Outside, prairie dogs leap onto Gus and bite down on his arm. His eyes bulge, but he somehow doesn't scream out in pain. He still makes plenty of noise. Loud hoots and yells. He yawps as he rips the prairie dogs off him and throws them back into the horde. He stomps them, squishing their bodies like cigarette butts. As they launch themselves at him, he grabs hold of their heads and squeezes down until blood squirts out from between his fingers. "Come on!" he yells out. "Come on!"

One scurries by his leg and rips away a large chunk of flesh. Gus drops to one knee as he yanks another dog off his shoulder. Several of them leap up behind him. He arches his back, cringing, but it barely slows him. Even when a prairie dog bursts out of his chest and hisses, his immediate reaction is to clap both hands down to crush its head.

Another dozen prairie dogs climb onto him and clamp down. He yanks off one and beats another with it. More still grasp onto his body. They crawl under his clothes and tear their way through him. They shred his bald spot. The one with the mohawk gnaws at his eye.

To that, he finally screams. He writhes and twists. Some of the prairie dogs fall. Some are thrown in random directions. He manages to aim several at the church door. I scream as they fly at me, but they burst into flames and ash as soon as they're inside.

I scramble back just the same. I can't manage to pull myself away from watching dozens of prairie dogs pounce onto Gus and rip him to pieces. But I find the view from behind the second pew is just as good as the doorway. It's too much too take in; I've never seen such a thing. I barely notice the three vampires standing in the yard, watching the chaos with delighted faces.

"My," Lianna chuckles over Gus's screams and grunts, "Your maker truly is a powerful one. I've never seen my babies work so hard to dispose of a body."

Leviathan walks to Gus. Practically strolls. Both arms are back, I notice. Gus must've dropped it when I fired the revolver. Apparently vampires can reattach their limbs. The same way Gus can get up after crashing through a roof. There's still a lot of gore caked around the wound. Veins and nerves are twisting, stabbing into his shoulder like stitches. He steps over the prairie dog army, many of which are standing or squatting on the lawn. Just like me, they're watching their brethren rip through Gus as he flails around, fighting back. Those he fends off don't seem too eager to get back into the fight. They move slowly, sluggishly. A couple clutch their bellies.

One vomits blood.

Others do the same. Not all the prairie dogs. Just the ones he's fended off. They all puke blood out onto the grass. I can't help but lean forward in my pew. It's horrible. It's disgusting. I know. But at this point it's just the kind of night I'm having. So I watch, honestly a little sympathetic. My heart goes out to bunches of murderous prairie dogs as they hurl blood all over the church lawn. I can't help it. They're objectively adorable.

A thing about the blood they're all vomiting is, it's not just splattering onto the grass or getting absorbed in the soil. It's pooling. It's gliding along the lawn, forming little rivers as it all directs back toward Gus.

Leviathan clearly doesn't notice. He continues his slow walk forward. Some of the blood glides right over his feet, and he pays no attention. He steps closer to Gus and says, "You seem in pain, friend. Does the agony overwhelm?"

Gus stops screaming. I can't even see him beneath all of the prairie dogs. They clamber and claw, forming a mound over his body. How he's able to speak, I can't imagine. And whatever he does say, I can't understand. I hear his voice though. Some words, sloppy and gargling. From the disgust on Leviathan's face, they must've hit home.

"You dare!" Leviathan screams. "You mother sucking-" instead of finishing his sentence, the rest of his reply comes in the form of a well placed kick, square in Gus's chest. Gus is thrown back from the impact, bouncing the church stairs. There are a few snaps. I'm not sure if they're bone or cement. Probably both. Gus makes a few more guttural sounds as Leviathan approaches. Gus crawls backwards up the steps, lifting an arm to shield himself from the vampire, even though it's covered in gnawing prairie dogs. It doesn't slow

Leviathan. He kicks again, knocking Gus to the top of the stairs. Gus tries to sit up. I have no idea how. But he puts up both hands and gargles out a couple of words. Leviathan snarls and lifts him up by the throat. He balls his fist, veins in his shoulder pulsing.

"No!" Lianna screams. "Wait!"

Leviathan doesn't wait. He uppercuts Gus in the jaw. Gus is launched into the church. As soon as he passes the doorway, the dozens of prairie dogs chomping down on him all burst into flames. He soars through the air like a comet, exploding when he hits the altar. Bones, charred hunks of flesh, and a few patches of unscathed meat come to rest at center stage. The moonlight from the stain glass windows create a silhouette of what's left of him, along with the ashes lingering in the air.

Outside, all three vampires rush toward the door. "What have you done?" Lianna screams.

"My babies!" Ellis yells out.

Many of the other prairie dogs also scamper up to the doorway and look inside. Among them, I see the larger one with the white mohawk, staring me down again. None of them cross the barrier.

"How could you?" Ellis screams at Leviathan, grabbing him by the back of the head, clutching a fistful of hair. Ellis shoves forward, forcing Leviathan's face into the doorway. Leviathan is able to turn his head, but the side of his face ignites. His ear, cheek, and brow all burn. He looks like a sparkler on the Fourth of July. His eyeball swells, then pops. Ocular fluid boils in the empty socket before evaporating.

"I'm sorry!" Leviathan screams. His arms scramble for something to grip onto, but there's only the open air of the church doorway. Tiny flames burst on his fingers as he struggles. "I'm sorry! I'm sorry!"

Eventually Ellis seems to grow tired of the torture and throws Leviathan back at the lawn. He bowls over some of the prairie dogs and comes to rest, clutching his face.

"You!" Ellis's voice deepens. He glares at me, nostrils flaring. His eye, the one I shot, isn't entirely reformed. It's a bundle of pulsing meat. I don't even know what. Maybe brains. I duck down into the pew. I think to run, but where? This is the safest I've been all night. So I lie in place as Ellis snaps, "What hell have you brought on our family? You murdered my son! You killed my babies. Come forth this instant! Reap the agony you've earned."

I murdered his son? I killed Charles? It hits me like a ton of bricks. I stabbed him in the side with a wooden stake. I hit his heart. Gus said it before, but with everything happening, the thought just sort of washed over me. I murdered someone. I took a life. Yes, my abductor. Yes, a man who-crazy as it sounds-killed me first. Just as the realization hits me, I have a million defenses and reasons. I didn't mean to kill him. He was evil. I was just trying to escape. It was self-defense. I can justify it to myself in every way imaginable. But to hear it, to know… I murdered someone. The weight of those words, the gravity of this entire night, it's all too much. How did I get from my first night in a ticket booth to here? The tears start to well. I try to fight back, to reign myself in. But it's all too much. All I can do is cover my mouth and sob.

"Come forth!" Ellis commands. Hundreds of prairie dogs bark at his words.

I won't. I can't. I just lie in the pew and weep.

"Human?" he stammers. "I told you to come forth!" He stomps his foot. "She should respond to my heed. Why is she not coming forth?"

After a moment, Lianna takes a turn. "Girlfriend?" she says with a palpable uncertainty. "I hear you sniffling. I'm sorry Ellis is being so cruel. I'm sorry you were offered to us. It's our culture, you see. We map out territories. It's for our own safety. When another vampire entered our lands, and offered you to us, that was entirely his actions. Not ours. We wouldn't have thought to hunt you on our own. Not a young, innocent women with her whole life ahead of her. Really, we only kill… Old, bad people. Monsters really."

I don't respond. I just let myself weep. This is hardly the time, some distant part of myself screams. Not while they're still here, speaking to me. Not with a dead man on the altar. But honestly there's nowhere else to go. Nothing I can do. The fact that I'm here, that this is happening. It's just too much.

She continues. "The ghoul who attacked us is dead. Whoever his master is, I can assure you, he will answer a hundred fold for the insult. Our fight is with him. Not you. We promise not to harm you. I'm sure you can imagine, we're full of questions. Just come out. Talk to us. Help us figure this out. Together."

Leviathan chimes in. "Yes. Please, my darling. Join us and no harm will come to you. I swear I can protect you from the bastard who offered you as a sacrifice." This from a man who who apparently chops women to bits and keeps their hair for souvenirs. Later, I'll think back and hate myself for this moment, because it works. Not that I suddenly trust my killers. Nothing in the world could make me approach them. But I'm tired. I'm stressed. I'm at the end of my rope. So with a face full of tears I sit up to scream, "Go! Just go away! Leave me-"

I don't have to feel Lianna's mind to realize she played me. She smirks something wicked. They're all grinning as she cocks back the hammer on Gus's revolver. Our eyes meet, and just for a second, I see her prairie dogs back in her home. I know them by name. Boxer. Shepard. Judas. Polaris. Harper. Sugar. Nessun. Mog. Hurley. Buttons. Spaz- that's the larger one with the white mohawk. And for some reason, that one makes her nervous. The list of names goes on and on. I know each of them who died when Gus was punched into the church. Fifty six prairie dogs died tonight, and Lianna remembers cutting and stitching capes for every single one of them. She thinks of how Ellis bit into their backs and drained them. How he'd pricked his finger, giving them his blood. They'd be revived in Lianna's loving hands. She'd coddle them as she tied on their capes and offered a mouse for them to feed on. They bred the things for years, charging them to protect their home.

I see a lifetime of pet care. I'd see more if not for the gun. I duck. The entire church flashes and accompanying thunder trembles its walls. A chunk of pew near my head explodes into dust. Holes burst into the next several pews. Lianna cackles over the ringing in my ears. "Holy shit!" she laughs. "Fucker kicks like a mule!"

From the altar, a gruff, gargling voice says, "Special gunpowder. Mix it m'self."

Several more shots boom through the church. I slide down the pew, as far from gunfire as I can get without showing myself. That voice was Gus.

I'm not the only one questioning. Dozens of prairie dogs chirp outside, which unfortunately doesn't drown out Leviathan screaming, "Suck off! I'll suck you up!"

He hears himself, right? I mean, how does he not hear himself?

Lianna fires again. "What the hell are you?" Her question is punctuated by another bullet.

Gus's voice becomes more clear with every word. "See, commercial powders are made fer killin' deer an' teenagers. Ya'll wanna put some holes in a werewolf, a basilisk, maybe some swamp man motherfucker, ya gotta get some kick. Personally, I like makin' charcoal outta grapevine, maple, and just a bit of willow fer that extra nudge. Little sulfur, and a whole lotta niter. I make m'own niter, ya know." I want to look up. I want to see him, still alive. Even after that hit. Even after… and I feel off just thinking it, but even after all those prairie dogs exploded around him. Thankfully after the last shot, I have enough sense to keep down.

Lianna fires another round, which encourages me to keep my head out of view. The gunshot doesn't deter his monologue. Despite probably taking several bullets, he's getting closer.

He continues, "See, long time ago we used ta make the niter outta piss n' cow flop. Well one day, some years back, I figured, shit. I ain't got no cows. But then I figured I got m'own flop factory right here and there's a burger joint just up the street."

He comes into view, dragging his feet more than walking down the center aisle of the church. It's horrible. The most recognizable parts of the man look like jerky. His flesh is charred with entire muscles ripped away. His left arm is stripped with muscle dangling off his bone, with his forearm dragging limply by his feet. I can see several ribs and what I know can't be his heart, but possibly his stomach sagging between them. A part of me, a very small part, can't help but look for a gallbladder. He pauses at my row, turning ever so slightly to face me. Oh God, he's naked. His clothes must've been incinerated in the blast. Of course there's only one part of him not burned beyond recognition.

Of all the things in the world.

After a wink and what very well could be a smile, he continues toward the vampires. “I don’t know if it’s m’diet or maybe that I’m some sorta ghoul, but damn if I don’t make a strong niter. An’ it don’ help with the killin’ ‘r nothin. I jus’ get a kick outta knowin’ when I put a bullet in someone, there’s at least some chance they got a bit o’ my burned up waste in there with it.” He stops at the vampires, standing in front of Ellis. I don’t even realize I’ve sat up to watch, transfixed on this walking corpse. But it’s more than that. Even in the dark of the church, I can make out little shifts and pops on his body. His arm is rising back up off the floor. His spine is straightening. Muscle fibers are twisting back into place. His skin lightens, the charred burns fading, returning to soft tissue. It’s like Gus is melting back together. Not like the vampires. There aren’t any weaving veins or pulsing flesh. He just reassembles. Not even fully formed, he leans over Ellis, right up to the very edge of the doorframe. “Point is,” he says. “When that there girly fired m’gun straight into yer face, ain’t no way in hell the gunpowder didn’t smear yer brains full a’ all sorts a’ little particles a’ my piss. An’ my shit. An’ it’s gonna stay right there. Long after yer done healing. Long after yer in the ground ta stay. From now on, no matter what you do, no matter where you go, ya’ll always got flecks o’ my shit in yer brain.”

There’s a deafening silence. Made worse by the ringing in my ears from all the gunfire. The raging heat from Ellis’s face can probably be felt for miles. But Gus doesn’t seem to notice. Instead he looks past Lianna, to Leviathan. “Say friend,” he asks in a casual tone. “Those pants o’ yers? They flame retarded?” He grabs Leviathan by the belt and yanks him forward, throwing him into the church. He laughs as Leviathan ignites into white hot flames. Leviathan burns to ash as Lianna and and Ellis scream. Gus doesn’t pay any attention. He just steps over Leviathan’s burning body and starts stomping the flames. His foot passes through easily, with thick clouds of lavender scented ashes puffing up around him. When the flames die out, he picks up the remains of Levi’s pants and chuckles to himself. He says, “heh, sucker” as he slips into Levi’s jeans.

“You monster!” Ellis is threatening as best he can. “Get out here. Come here this instant and face me!”

Lianna is on her knees with bloody tears rolling down her face. She's screaming for her fallen brother, heartbroken and enraged.

Gus looks me over, his face mostly returned to its original condition. Not that I'd call it an improvement, but at least he's healed. "Say, uh, Millie, right?" He speaks softly, combing ash out of his beard with his fingers. "Got a few hours 'til sunrise. There's here's a church. Bound ta be booze somewhere." He heads deeper into the church and, reluctantly, I follow.

I seat myself in what's either an office or a rectory. I'm not sure if there's a distinction. There had been a non-denominational church on the base growing up, but that was just a room connected to the rec center. And I'd only ever been there with friends. Maybe once or twice with Dad. Most of my religious upbringing had been from Mama's occasional references to the Torah, which she always seemed to think I knew in spite of having only been to Temple as a little kid. Truthfully, the only thing I can say for certain about either of the religions my parents failed to expose me to is that, on important days, I should probably light a candle. So, sitting here, I know a priest's private chamber is called a rectory. But shouldn't there be a bed or small shrine or something? Or would they need a shrine when literally the entire building is one? There is a picture of Jesus Christ on the far wall. Maybe that counts.

The room has a desk, a few bookshelves, some chairs, and there's an old worn-out sofa by the door. It's not the most comfortable thing in the world, but it beats the pew. Especially under gunfire.

I take ten or twenty minutes to sit in silence and ponder everything that's happened since I was yanked from the theater. Some of my more basic conclusions come with little effort. Honestly, I should be way past them but a lot of what I've seen just won't settle. Mostly because it's the sort of stuff that shouldn't settle. Even after my cry, after feeling physically and emotionally drained, none of it settles. Vampires exist. They seem to like prairie dogs. I am now a ghoul to one. But I killed him. Vampire blood healed my wounds, and I think made me telepathic. I've killed someone.

I drove a wooden stake into the side of his heart and took his life.

He killed me first, or at least brought me to the brink of death. It was self-defense. But I killed him. I killed him. I replay that stab again and again. I was his victim. I feel victimized. Not just for everything leading up the moment, but because of it. There was a side of myself I never wanted to know. Never should've had to know.

Yesterday I was anxious over bills and restarting my relationship. Now I'm a second-degree murderer.

Gus walks into the rectory holding two bottles of wine in one hand. He lights a few random candles. A thought occurs to me, so I stare in an attempt to read his mind. It doesn't work. I try squinting and staring at his head. That doesn't work either. Oh well. He sits at the desk and our eyes meet. Suddenly I see myself naked, sweaty, squeezing his pecker between my significantly larger breasts. I look away, mortified.

He says, "What?" So it seems the mind thing only works through eye contact. And he can't tell when I'm perceiving his thoughts. I can't decide if that's a good or a bad thing.

"I...um," I stutter, "thank you for saving me from them, I think."

"Least I could do," he says, biting the cork off one bottle and taking a gulp. He scratches the side of his head and a few ashes flake out of his hair. "I gotch'ya yer own bottle." He offers me the one with the cork still on it.

"No thanks. I don't drink."

He shrugs, bites the cork off the second bottle, and takes a swig. "Churches always make me drink," he says. He sets the two bottles next to each other. Neither is empty, but I'm certain it won't be long before they both are. We sit in silence a few more minutes. He chugs half a bottle. "So," he finally says. "Ya'll probly got a question er two."

Before I even fully form the thought, I ask, "How are there vampires?"

He shrugs. "How's there you n' me? Always been vampires. Always been werewolves. Always been fuckin' chupacabras runnin' 'round the fuckin' place. Jus' not many I s'pose." Our eyes meet and another image invades my mind. Now Gus is being given a blow job by some sort of strange lizard dog creature. I look away and image is gone, but the memory will probably always remain. As I rub my eyes, he returns to his bottle for a couple of swigs and says, "Now vampires is –well- kinda the faggots o' the unnatural world. Err. Maybe the fags o' the supernatural world. Hunderd, maybe two hunderd years ago, vampires was what they called a formidable fuckin' opponent. Used to be ruthless as sin. Kinda creatures that rip out-cher heart n' drink' it empty while ya watch. Used ta slaughter off man fer the fun o' it. Used ta be, being a vampire meant you was the toughest, baddest beast around. They got soft though. Fuckin' weak n' faggy in ev'ry regard. Must'a been when I killed off all them old ones. The others ain't got nothin' ta teach 'em right no more."

Ugh. I hate that word. *Faggot. Fag. Faggy.* With everything else, every time he says it, a little piece of my patience gets picked away. I want to call him out over his vulgarities, but this is hardly the time. Prairie dogs and murderers are probably surrounding the building. Worst comes to worst, I'll just have to deal with him until sunrise. I can keep it together that long. Instead of reminding him how horrible he is, I keep the discussion on vampires. "What do you mean?" I ask.

"I got ideas 'bout it," Gus says before taking another drink. "Them werewolves don' care. Dragons don' care. Zombies sure as shit don' care. They just is. They do as they do 'cause they're fuckin' dragons n' zombies n' werewolves. Ain't got no mind. They jus' like any other wild animal. Vampires –n' I don't know if ya'll e'er heard a vampires before- but see the thing with them is they used ta be men. N' women. Some o' pertier ones used to be women. But they still got brains innum. Still think like men. Still act like men. N' all these fuckin' vampires think they gots all the time in the world. So when they ain't out doin' vampire things they all sitting 'round doin' man-stuff. Like watchin' TV. Or readin' books. I like to read some too. Not no fuckin' vampire books. Not no more. They all 'bout fuckin' love stories n' girl problems n' fallin' in love n' shit. You know, dumb bitches n' getting' off n' bullshit. Anyways, on toppa l'il girls n' lonely faggots, them vampires also enjoy reading them vampire books. Then them vampires like them books, and they even start actin' like them books. They start wearin' leather n' baggy shirts. Some o' them put on make-up n' make themselves look more pale. Wear fuckin' sunglasses at night. That kinda bullshit. Vampires see better than people n' all, but I can't tell ya how many I killed jus' sneaking up on 'em. Or how many tried to flee n' bumped inta somethin' er other. Fuckin' sunglasses." He pauses for another swig of wine. "Back there, we had ourselves four kinds a vampire. We had a classic, we had a psycho leather-bitch, we had a teen heartthrob, and if I had to guess, I'd say the one you killed was a *Tom Cruise*."

The one I killed. "Tom Cruise? The actor?" I'm not exactly a fan, but I think over the few of his movies I've seen. One of them was *Interview with a Vampire*. "Don't you mean a *Lestat*?" I ask, thinking of Tom Cruise's character in the film.

"Nah," he says. "I seen this before. They like that movie, but always end up dressin' n' actin' like the actor. Him err Elvis. Some select women vampire always try ta be like that there uh Betty White. Don' know why. Friendly as shit though. I almost feel bad puttin' 'em down."

"Why do you then?" I ask.

"They're vampires," Gus says with another swig of the bottle. "Ye need a better reason?"

"Is that what you do then? For a living, I guess. You're a vampire hunter?"

Gus shrugs. He chugs his bottle some more. "I hunt," he says, "vampires n' anything else that thinks it might be bigger n' me. I hunt all sorts o' fuckers though. Far as what I am is concerned, back there ya mighta heard the word *ghoul* being tossed around. Never thought of it that way, but I spose it's fair ta say as much."

"Is that why you came back to life? Ghouls can't be killed?"

"Nah. Most ghouls die pretty quick. Ghouls is just creatures serving the creature possessin' o'er 'em."

"Oh. So are you like a warrior with God or the church or something? Is that why you're…" The question trails off. I don't have words for whatever he is.

Gus laughs. "Of fuck no. Trust me, girl. God ain't got nothin' ta do with me. I'm jus' what I am 'cause the creature who done made me is so strong."

"Oh?" I wait for him to continue. Instead he wipes away a tear, chuckling to himself. I ask, "What was it? The creature that made you?"

That seems to sober him. Or at least his laughter. He takes a swig from one of the bottles and lets the wine sit in his mouth before swallowing. He says "My wife."

I let the idea breathe a moment before asking, "Okay. What kind of creature is your wife?"

"A cunt."

Ugh. I hate that word too. Of course he'd use it. But, then again, looking at this bear of a man as he downs two bottles of wine during a break from his battle with vampires and prairie dogs, I think, maybe. Just maybe. At a minimum, if his wife turns out to be some sort of giant flapping vagina monster, I probably shouldn't be surprised. I wonder if she'd fly or glide along like a stingray. And if she has fangs. On that note, I decide to change the subject. "Am I a ghoul? Like you?"

Our eyes meet and I see that image of myself again, stabbing Charles in the side and making a run for it. It's different in Gus's mind. He feels bemused and fascinated. Jealous, I think. "Nah. You got the smell o' death in ya all right. But no ghoul ne'er killed its master before. Can't be done, far as I know. I ne'er can. When ya kill a vampire, its ghouls always b'come human again. The magic betwixt 'em dies. I don' know how ya'll did whachya did, but it's the most impossible thing since trying ta give yerself anal. Once a vampire gets a hold on a ghoul, ya like its own sock puppet. We're talkin' fist up yer ass. You don' breathe 'less they let you. It's perty amazin.' Breakin' control like that. I been wantin' ta ask since we got outside the house, but how'd ya do it? How'd ya overpower yer maker like that?"

I have no idea. "Maybe he was just distracted." I say. Gus is dissatisfied by the explanation. He replays the moment. Over and over, he recalls me stabbing Charles. One second I'm lying limp on the floor. The next I'm running for the window, Charles crumbling in my place. He wants to see something deeper. He's irked my explanation makes sense. "God. That's so weird," I utter to the vision of myself in his mind.

"What's weird?" Gus says. "And I'll thank ya ta not be cursin' o'er the Lord in his own home."

Oh. Of course *he* calls me out for *my* language. I don't say it, but considering he said God had nothing to do with him, and he just said *cunt*, I find his restriction of *me* saying *God* a bit puzzling. I continue watching me murder Charles over and over in Gus's mind. As the vision repeats, I notice how my clothes are more tattered. My chest is exposed. Over and over. I say, "Could you to stop trying to imagine me with larger boobs?"

Gus grins. He looks away, breaking the vision. He doesn't seem embarrassed. More amused than seconds from blushing. "Ye got some a yer master's power," he says. He leans in, looks straight into my eyes and says, "Well that don' matter none. I wan' ya ta forget evrythin' ya'll seen tonight."

Even from across the desk, he's too close for comfort. I lean away. I tell him, "I don't think I can forget."

"Huh?" Gus slaps both hands onto the desk. "Hold up a sec. Let me try again." He blinks a few times and clears his throat. He looks me in the eyes and says without any accent, "You will forget everything from tonight."

"No," I say. "How?"

"Wait," Gus says. "I can't control ya? Ya don' feel me controlling ya from within yer soul or any o' that shit? Not even a l'il?"

"Um? No."

"That's so weird," he says. "Ye sure? Get nekkid."

"No!"

He tilts his head like a puzzled dog. "Yeah, I guess so," he says. "Well, don' worry none. Prolly wear off in time."

"How much time?"

He shakes his head. "Ya jus' seein' shit er pickin' up on feelings too?"

"Like, emotions or physical sensations? When Charles… The one I killed, when I was drinking his blood I felt… both. Definitely both."

"Oh," Gus nods. After a moment he says, "Well, ya killed 'im so it's likely to go away."

Now I'm the one who's dissatisfied. We sit in a silence, or at least not speaking while he gulps down Communion wine. I try to find some words, but none come to mind. Truthfully, I don't want to speak to him. I don't want him anywhere near me. If all the evil in the world wasn't outside right now, I'd run screaming. Now that I can run.

I study the stitches on my leg. They're crossing over the wound in a zigzag, but the injury itself is healed. It's just a white scar, paler than the rest of my pasty leg. To think vampires can do this to a person. The implications aren't lost on me. Think of how the world would be different if hospitals hooked people up to IVs of vampire blood. Of course, insurance probably wouldn't cover it under some risk or clause. And vampire blood is significantly rarer than human blood. So a bag of the stuff would definitely cost thousands. So I'd still be in debt. Maybe not as much if I'd gotten a transfusion prior to having my gallbladder removed.

From this moment and for most of my life, I wonder if Charles's blood caused my gallbladder to grow back. And why he couldn't have murdered me before I had the thing removed.

A prairie dog perches on the windowsill outside the office/rectory room. Gus sees it and makes a noise, somewhere between a grunt and what might be a threat. He flips the desk up onto its end, shimmies it over the window, then shoves a bookcase against it. He obstructs the view. He scrambles around the office, shoving bookshelves, the Jesus painting, and whatever else he can find until he's satisfied the window is covered. "Well this ain't going well at all," he says, flopping onto the far side of the sofa. "Everythin' since the helicopter done fell apart."

It takes a moment to remember what he's talking about. The fact that a police helicopter crashed into the vampire's house while hundreds of prairie dogs stood poised to kill me, at this point, feels like a footnote. "Oh yeah," I say. "Where did that come from?"

"I fuckin' stole it," Gus says. "Went to the police station ta get m'knife. They was landing it while I was showin' up n' I thought, 'I want that helicopter.' So I took it. Flew it o'er that theater you was at. When that vampire took ya, he was movin' pretty fast. But I just followed the trail o' blood ya left. Took me right to 'em. Then when I saw yer blood start poolin' into the house, I knew they was turnin' ya. Makin' you a ghoul or a vamp. So I intervened."

"My blood was going into the house? Like yours? I don't remember that."

"You was prolly dead a few minutes there n' didn't notice much o' anything. You was usin' crutches before n' are walkin' just fine now, right? Along with the vampire blood, ya got a lot o' yers back. Somethin' 'bout the rebirth. I don' get it. Point is really I got to jump outta helicopter n' crash a vampire party. How often do I get ta say that?"

How Gus fell through the ceiling starts to make sense. But as I'm playing back the events of the evening, it occurs that the first vampire attacked me because of whatever Gus dumped in the street. That's why I was yanked out of the theater. Whatever it was Gus dumped from his cup drove Charles insane. "Wait," I say. Everything starts coming back. "The vampires said I was offered. Like a sacrifice or a gift or something. Why did they think that?" I look into Gus's eye as I ask.

He says, "Well, uh," and trails off. But I'm seeing everything. Wyanet sits at the bar alone. I smell the hint of lavender from her body lotion. And another odor. Faint, familiar, musky and sweet. Vaginal. Gus's thoughts show a chain of youthful, lustful women, all of them in pain. Virgins. He remembers virgins. Wyanet sits at the bar alone. He sees me across the room, through the mirror. He looks to Wyanet and says, "Ya miss 'er, don't ya?"

Gus's eyes widen as he looks away. "Now don't you go creepin' 'round m'head. Some thing ya prolly ain't meant to see."

I snap. "You were stalking me! What were you doing? Why?"

He stammers. "Now, girl, don't go-" I don't pay attention. He looks away so I stand and circle around. I angle myself to him. He glances. I catch a glimpse of him in a dark room. It's familiar. It's Candace's bedroom!

Gus shuts his eyes. "You were with Candace! You were in my home!" I push him. He glares at me. Suddenly I'm back in my apartment. Gus is staring down at Candace and I. He's telling us, "*Now why don' ya bring your friend back ta...*" He sniffs. He smells me? "*You a virgin*?" I feel the plan forming. The vampires in town. Always so distant in the air. But virgin blood. My blood. Why does he keep thinking I'm a virgin? He says, "*Ne'er mind, girls. Ya'll forget I was e'er here. We gonna have some fun. We gonna have all sorts o' fun.*" We stare blankly back. He does the same thing to us that

Charles did to me at the theater. But instead of controlling me, he makes me forget.

"You did this! You did everything! All because you think I'm a virgin!"

"What? What'd ya see?" Gus shakes his head. He pushes me back. Not hard, but it doesn't take much effort to make me stumble to the far wall. "Look. Shit! Jus' shit," he keeps his face low. "First fuckin' bead o' light I seen in a fuckin' century n' already yer fuckin' with m' head." He punches his own leg. "All right. We gonna be stuck here a spell. Might as well jus' fuckin' tell ya. Jus' shit! Jus' calm the fuck down n' Lemme explain."

I don't sit. I demand to know, "You screwed my roommate and were about to hypnotize me into sex! Why were you with her? What is going on?"

"Jus' sit down n' shut yer fuck hole n' I'll tell ya."

"Excuse me?" I scream.

Keeping his head low, he slams both fists into his legs. There's a crunch. I think he just broke his own legs, which is the only thing that makes me pause. "Millie, shut the fuck up and sit yer ass down!"

The top of his head flushes pink. The veins in his arms and neck are all pulsing. A wave of anxiety is enough to make me settle. Only for a moment. In the back of my mind I tell myself that this isn't over and whatever he has to say had better be good. I back away. I don't sit though. I lean on the wall.

He lifts his head enough to look my way, but without making eye contact. "Shit. Ya know all that? Shit. Okay. Kinda starts 'bout two r' three months ago. I got this gorgon girl I fuck sometimes. Anyways, last time I was in her neck 'o the woods, she got herself a vampire problem. Fuckin' blood suckers moved into the city n' killin' all the locals. She can't have it 'cause it draws attention n' well, she got snakes fer hair n' occasional visitors already turn ta stone n' shit. So she don' need no attention."

I say, "Get to the part where you screwed my roommate-" but he talks over me.

"So I stalk the vampire fer ever. Just one. Just one measly li'l leather clad faggot. Couldn't even turn ta bats r' nothin.' Anyways, I got 'im pinned. 'Bout to stake this broken broom handle so far up his ass, it makes his heart gush. N' he's beggin' fer his life 'r after-life 'r whatever the fuck. Tells me if I let him live, he'll point me ta hunderds o' vampires. He knows him a gaggle o' vampires so big that ain't no other vampires can live n' the North. I kill all them, it'll give him plenty country to roam. Plenty of places to feed without drawin' attention 'r creatin' problems. So I make like we got a deal. He says Kalamazoo. I stake his dumb ass. Of all the fuckin' places fer there ta be vampires. I got kin up this way. M'brother's descendants live in the area. So I make m' way North. Sure enough, this whole town smells o' vampire. E'ery rotten inch. Like more vampire than anybody'd e'er be able ta hide. Problem is- where the fuck is they?" He throws up his arms in a grand gesture of the question. "I'm smellin' so much vampire I gotta bury m' nose in goat ass jus ta get fresh air. And n' the outskirts o' town ya got some common burial grounds n' whathave. But only a couple o' bodies here n' there. Most is just ripped up pieces. So ain't just the air. Ain't no trickery. There's vampires all o'er the fuckin' place. Town oughta be bleedin' vampire, it got so much stink. But I couldn't find none. Decided the only way ta get to 'em was ta smoke 'em out."

"Virgin blood," I whisper. "They were excited because they thought I was a virgin-"

"Can you believe my luck?" he says, cutting me off yet again. "This here a college town. I figure them vampires is tryin' to blend in. Takin' night classes. Goin' to the bars fer a li'l carry out. So I'm scopin' the neighborhood, lookin' fer their hives. An' there comes walkin' this blonde tease. Yer roommate. Well, maybe she's lookin' fer a good time. An' I'm havin' a shit night. So I suggest pretty hard, we go have a good time together. Wouldn't worked if she weren't jus' a bit interested. Jus' sayin.' So I'm 'bout to get goin' n' that's when I smell ya. Like a bottle o' 1787 Chateau Lafitte jus' rolled out n' humped m'leg. Not that ya'd drink' nothin' that old, but ya get my point. Virgin blood."

The machete in my leg. The mop bucket. "You used my blood as bait," I snarl. "Because it smells virginal."

"Well ya'll is a virgin, ain't ya?"

My impulse is to scream, "That's none of your business!" but instead I just grumble, "No. I've been having sex for years."

He smirks like a schoolboy. “Oh come on. You ain’t never had no dick.”

“I’ve had…” I stutter. I connect the dots. That has to be the absolute lamest technicality ever. “That can’t be right. Just because I’ve only been with women? That’s what makes my blood the perfect bait?”

“No! No. Well, yeah. Jus’ not entirely. I find the perfect bait is a mixture o’ blood n’ ol’ family recipe barbeque sauce. Vampire can’t eat no human food, but they sure love the smells.”

I don’t need to look into his eyes to piece the rest together. Gus needed *virgin* blood. He stalked me. I catch myself rubbing a hand over the ridge of my machete scar. The stitches pull as my finger grazes over them. “How?” I asked, replaying the memory of that frat boy slipping with the knife. “How could you have possibly done that?”

Gus shrugs. “I just got a way. S’pose I coulda jus hypnotized it outta ya, but there weren’t no challenge init. Got the puddle, the bartender so he’d pull o’er the bucket fer me ta collect. Real trick was yer little dyke friend you was pining o’er. Bloods better when it got them pheromones init. Love juice. Been watchin’ ya watchin’ her watchin’ ya. Ya’ll both a couple o’ pussies, by the way. What I’m sayin’ is, I gave the girl the nudge ya both needed. So what it all comes down ta is, I brought ya li’l girl fags back ta-gether fer jus’ a bit o’ blood. So no need ta thank me. We’re square. An’ yer welcome.”

“You bastard!” I scream. I rush him. “How could you do that to me? How could you do that to her? Because of a couple of vampires? You- you bastard!” I’m back in swinging distance and making the most of it. Everything is white, hot fire as I punch, scream, and pull away clumps of his hair. How could he? How! He coerced my roommate into sex. He tricked Wyanet into loving me. He made fools of us! He brought monsters to my door and they killed me! They killed me! I scream, punch, and smash his face in.

He tolerates it. “Not jus’ a couple o’ vampires, Millie,” he says far, far too casually as I beat him. “Hunderds o’ vampires. Hunderds of fanged murderous night creatures that done gorge themselves on the blood ‘o man. Had I known most o’ them was prairie dogs, I prolly woulda handled matters different.”

“Everything is a lie!” I hit him. Over and over, I hit him. It doesn’t leave an impact. Blood spurts and bruises, but he couldn’t care less. Which makes me want to hit him harder. To show him all the damage he’s done. I thought I had Wyanet back. I thought we were working things out. I can’t even wrap my head around him with Candace. He raped her! Even having been in his mind, I don’t know how much was him tricking her, and how much was her, but the fact that he pushed her at all means she wasn’t in control. For both of them. For me. It’s all too much. I need him to hurt.

“Half lies, really," His tone is mildly defensive. He feels nothing for what he’s done. I could break him a thousand different ways and he wouldn’t bat an eye. He doesn’t care. Not one bit.

The room rumbles.

I lose my balance and fall to the floor. The entire room shakes. Gus spits away some blood. His teeth rattle on the sofa, then zip back into his mouth. "Earthquake?" he says. "'Round here?"

The entire room rattles. The furniture, piled around the window, all starts to collapse. I try to stand, but slip and sprawl across the floor. The whole room drops a foot and Gus slides off the sofa, onto his back. His head cracks the tile. "What-" I can't finish the question. Everything is shaking. I flail my arms, reaching for something, anything to grip onto.

"Hang on, girl!" Gus screams. In an instant I'm swooped back in his arms, over his shoulder. He kicks the office door open. "Ah. Hell!” He grunts, sliding through the hall and back into the church. Pews are jostling around. All of them have fallen over. All of the stain glass windows shatter. "Hang on, girl! Hang on!" He darts into the chaos. The altar collapses into a pit. The pipe organ spills into the hole. Gus yells, “We ain’t gonna make it!” as bricks spill from the walls. Everything rumbles and the floor splits beneath his feet. “It’s cavin’ in!” Gus yells as he throws me forward.

I scream. I reach out for him. Not for him but a handhold to cling to as I’m propelled forward. He drops along with the floor. He screams, fighting to run just one more step before the rafters crush down on him. Gus screams, “Shit!” And just like that, he’s gone. Something grabs hold of me, pulling me from the wreckage.

"Look what I found!" Lianna cackles. She shoves me to my knees, holding me by the throat. She hisses and spittle patters my nose. I wince. It's just as frightening as it is awkward. Sure, it's scary. The fangs, her serpent voice. But what kind of person hisses? Maybe it's something vampires are more used to. For me there's a bit of culture shock. More so when she sniffs me. "Oh, such a sweet little blood bag you are." she laughs. "You thought you could hide? Safe, away from us in the haven of a little God? Well, my babies had something to say about that!" She lifts me in one hand, spinning me to face the rubble. The church is gone, replaced with heaps of planks, bricks, and tiles. All around, caped prairie dogs peep their heads up out of the ground. They squeak to one another in a chirpy chorus. They must've dug beneath the church. All of them. They created a sinkhole and brought down the entire building. "Now, as for your ghoulish friend," Lianna laughs. "Where is that fucking piece of shit?"

Ellis floats over the rubble, holding Gus's gun. He sniffs with a fanged grin on his face. "He… is… right…" He aims the gun beneath him. There's a loud creak and some of the rubble bursts out. A burly hand grabs Ellis by the heel, then yanks him out of view.

"What?" Lianna screams. She shoves me back onto the ground. "Father? Father!"

The chirping among the prairie dogs softens. Some of them approach the rubble. The one with the mohawk, Spaz, inches forward, sniffing.

Shrapnel bursts up from the ground. Gus leaps from the rubble, Ellis trapped in his arm. Gus holds a shard-err, stake-at his side, poised over the old man's chest. "Drop. The. Dyke!" He commands, blood seeping up his legs and back into his body. Splinters and stones pluck themselves from his face as he heals. Some get caught in his beard. Cuts and bruises heal over a few seconds. His one eye remains bloodshot. "Drop 'er or I stick a new fuck hole into yer daddy's heart." He stabs the spike an inch into Ellis's chest. There's a small spurt and blood drains from the wound, trickling down his tattoos, pooling at the rim of his pants. Our eyes meet and I see myself. Ellis is imagining his fingers gouging through my face, tearing my head apart, and ripping my entire body in half. My brain falls like a glob of Jell-o, and he punts it into a wall.

That's-That's really a lot to imagine while being stabbed. But he doesn't waver. He seems oblivious to the pain. "Rip her throat out!" He commands Lianna. He gnashes his teeth together, then swivels around in an effort to bite Gus. It's an awkward attack.

He manages to turn his head enough, but Gus just squeezes harder. He headbutts Ellis, right in the mouth. Ellis snarls as a fang and several other teeth drip from his face, into the rubble. Gus twists the stake, a boyish grin on his face. As Ellis squirms, Gus says, "What's it gonna be? Ya wanna watch me punish yer old man here or are ya gonna give me my dyke?"

Lianna's hand tightens the back of my throat. Prairie dogs are barking and hissing all around us. They're frantic, wanting to attack, but not advancing.

"Come on," Gus says. "This goes two ways. I ain't standin' down fer no faggy vampire. You either drop the dyke or we kill each other's bitches and I skull fuck you and all yer rodent friends 'til sunrise. Yer choice."

Lianna shoves me down a little harder. Some of the prairie dogs are standing on their hind legs, fangs bared at my face. One sticks out its tongue in its effort to taste me. I struggle. I try to inch away, but her grip is so strong. She just holds me there. After far too long she says, "Your master. I want to meet your fucking master."

"My mas…" Gus trails off, a small grin on his face. "Is that all?"

"If you want your waif back alive, you'll bring me the vampire who created you. I'll settle terms with him. I want to meet the fool who orchestrated this madness. I want the one who brought ruin to my home."

Gus squints. Our eyes meet, and from within him, there's a sort of cackling. I see black sky. Fiery eyes gleeful as they stare down from nothing. A single finger stirs Gus's entrails around on some rocks. I feel his screams in my lungs until I have to look away. "Okay," he smiles. "Okay. Ya'll want *the master*. We can make that happen. Why the fuck not? But I gotta fetch her."

"Take me to her," Ellis says.

"Nah. I gotta bring her to you. Might take some time. Here's how we'll do this. You take the girly. I'll take daddy. He'll speak to m'master fer ya and we'll all meet up again."

"Where?"

Gus shrugs. "Rooftop. Yeah. Earlier I saw this rooftop with a helipad. The tallest building in town. We'll meet up there. Twenty minutes before dawn. *The master* always appreciates a good view and a hint o' the morning light before daybreak."

Lianna is silent for a long moment. "Very well," she says. "Rooftop of the Hotel Renaissance. But if I so much as think there's any trickery afoot…"

"Yeah, yeah," Gus nods. "Same here. Ya'll kill the girl. I'll do worse to this one." He shakes Ellis, gyrating. But with that image burning a hole in my eyes forever, he pulls the spike from Ellis's chest and relaxes his grip. "Come on," he says. "M'truck's parked a few blocks from 'ere." He starts walking away, indifferently kicking several of the prairie dogs aside as he departs.

Ellis looks back. He tightens his fists, but Lianna shakes her head. He scowls. As they clear through the horde of prairie dogs, Gus relaxes his grip, walking with an arm around his shoulder. He's saying something, but I can't make out the words. He sounds cheerful.

Ellis glances back again. I notice the spidery lines of tattoos pointing down his shoulder blades. They all culminate at the small of his back, where a black widow spider is inked. I finally connect, all of his tattoos are meant to be spider webs.

"As for you…" Lianna says. She squeezes down on my throat. She's choking me. Killing me! I struggle. I flail my arms, hitting hers. But there's no… no…

I seize into a little ball and cough. Every hack for breath makes my head throb. Tears are pooling. I can't see. Where are my glasses? Where am I?

A chorus of squeaks and barks surrounds me. I hack out my lungs and the prairie dogs seem to bark at every noise I make. Prairie dogs.

"Awake I see?" Lianna says from somewhere nearby. I feel the wind. We're still outside. It's colder. I'm on cement.

"Glasses?" I cough.

"Ah! Yes. They fell off whilst I carried you. But I believe…" she trails off.

Little claws press my back. Between them something jabs at me. I roll onto my back and a small blur crawls onto my belly. It sets down my glasses. I slip them on. The blur becomes Spaz, cocking his head as he regards me. For some reason I think to thank him, but our eyes meet. He's chilly and contemplating nesting in my brain for warmth. So I say nothing. He barks and scampers off, blending into the crowd of prairie dogs that surrounds me. They're everywhere, forming a giant ring. All of them are chilly. Many are hungry. They don't like being up this high. We're on a rooftop. It's still night. Lianna stands near the ledge, looking down at the city. She holds an enormous, two-handed sword. It looks massive in her willowy arms. Ridiculous bordering on cartoonish. The weight of it should crush her. Yet, she seems to wield it without any trouble.

She glances over her shoulder at me and smirks. I notice a tattoo peeking up at her hip, just above the belt. Spider legs. It's a black widow. I thought vampires were immortal. Wouldn't a tattoo vanish? How old and ancient is she to have a tattoo in the first place? I think to ask, but instead I just stand. I take in the city around us. All five blocks of downtown Kalamazoo. The universities are to the West. North and East are small stretches of suburbs followed by miles of woods and farmland. "Wait," I say. "Did you knock me out to carry me to the top of the Renaissance Hotel?"

She doesn't answer. Instead she says, "I've never been up here. It's quite lovely, isn't it?"

I tell her, "I knew where we were going! I walk by here all the time. Did you think I was going to try to escape after all that? From a prairie dog army?"

She shrugs. "We flew. I assumed your screaming would convince me to drop you."

I see another truth in her eyes. "That's not at all what happened. You glammered some bellhop named Chaz into taking nine trips for all your prairie dogs. On the way up he asked if you wanted breakfast recommendations and you hissed at him like a cat. You can float a little but Ellis is the only one that flies and you're jealous- because you made him?"

She gives me the same hiss. I catches glimpses of her life, after she was turned. She loved it. The power that comes from being a huntress. But over the years she'd still visit him. She'd return to her father. In prisons? His hair went gray. He grew wrinkles. Her mom passed and he would die on the inside. Mourning her mom, she gave her dad a new life. One that, as it turns out, involves him really loving classic vampire movies.

I can't help it. I say, "Gus was right! Vampires are- You're in love with your own mythology! Your dad turned himself into Dracula!"

Is it wrong to think there's something cute about Ellis acting like a dad vampire? Being a father to her in that old man, dorky sort of way? I don't say this. At most I have a little pang of jealousy over it. I loved my dad, more than I resented him. I never would've done what Lianna had.

In a blink I'm back on the ground with a sword tipped to my throat. Lianna bares her fangs. "What of it?" she screams. "You think that makes us weak? Frail? Go on. Say it! Say I don't terrify you enough. Say I'm not the beast you imagined as a child, looming in the shadows, waiting to strike from beneath your bed."

It seems I've found a touchy subject. If not for the incredibly sharp blade at my jugular, I might say her family should just be themselves without trying to represent an image society projected on them. It really isn't the best time for that discussion though. I suppose the counter argument is that if they're happy celebrating themselves as vampires, no one has the right to deny them that. Yeah. I should leave it at that. "It's just culture shock. I'm out of sorts. I didn't mean to offend you."

Lianna's gaze goes from menacing to baffled to amused. She draws the sword away with a small chuckle. "You're something else," she says. "I'm kind of glad that ghoul shit didn't work out. Months of you around. You murdered my fucking brothers, bitch. You think I give a flying fuck about culture shock?" She paces. She rubs her fangs with her tongue. The prairie dogs chirp and bark all around her. "First, whoever that vampire is that caused all this shit. I'm killing him first chance I get. I don't even care about why he offered you or any of that shit. Half my family is gone. My babies are dead. He just needs to die. Then that hick ghoul of his after he's lost all his powers. You, I'm saving for last." She pauses, gazing off into the city. "It's just fucking beautiful up here, isn't it?"

I don't know why I say it. Especially after all that. Maybe because misery loves company. Maybe it's Stockholm Syndrome or just because we're both having such a bad night. But I tell her, "I hope you win. I don't want to die. But I'm rooting for you."

She laughs. "What?"

"Gus put me here. He's manipulated my life for weeks. He tricked me. Everyone I love, probably. He used me to get to you." I want to explain it all. To tell her that before the church came crashing down on top of us, I'd lost it. I was beating Gus as hard as I could and he couldn't have cared less. To go into every detail and explain, in just a few hours of knowing them all, with every attempt on my life, she's still the lesser of two evils. Or at least she cares about her dad. That's something. More than I can say for Gus. "I hope when he gets here, you actually can punish him. I doubt you'll be able to." I sigh. I tell her, "he's not fetching some master. Whatever that thing is he's a ghoul to, it's not around. When he shows up, things are going to get worse for you. I can pretty much promise that. But for what it's worth, my entire life is a joke. More so because of him. So I'll be rooting for you."

Her eyes thin. She doesn't believe me. She thinks it's some game I'm playing to trick her into sparing my life.

"S'pose I deserve that," Gus says. Lianna and all the prairie dogs whip their heads toward him. He's standing by the access door, alone, holding a duffle bag at his side. "I mean, damn girl. It ain't like I didn't get ya laid 'r nothin'. I get it, but damn."

Lianna poises her sword at him in one hand. "Where is Ellis? Where is your master?"

"Oh, daddy's close by," Gus says. "He's real fuckin' close. Far as masters go, I ain't seen mine in some years now. Wouldn't even know how ta call 'er."

"What?" Lianna gives me a sharp look.

Gus strolls forward. Not a care in the world. The bag bobs against his knee. It's white with black lines. Just a simple sack with a drawstring he has coiled around his hand several times. There's something familiar about it. I can't place it though. I definitely don't remember him with a bag earlier tonight. "Lemme tell ya how this is gonna work. Right now, ya got oh 'bout twenty minutes b'fore sunup. And I ain't fought myself a real vampire in quite some time. Yer friends weren't nothing ta speak of, but I bet you been around enough to get in a good one-two. So we gonna fight. N' either I kill you n' yers right here, right now. Or you'll beat me down enough ta escape b'fore daybreak. Ya'll win, I'll give ya a week ta clear outta town. Before I come fer ya again. An' believe you me. I won't never stop comin' fer ya."

Lianna snarls. To her prairie dogs she screams, "Kill him!"

The prairie dogs start to lunge, but Gus holds up the bag. "Wait!" He commands, and the prairie dogs freeze. Several of them bark. Others bare their fangs and hiss. Gus smirks at the sack. "We do this my way 'r you'll never see ol' pappy again!" There's a lot of snarling among the crowd. Many look back and forth between Lianna and Gus. He says, "Ya'll wanna walk outta here with 'im? Ya gotta earn his life."

Lianna raises her sword "Where is he?"

Gus swings the sack around and tosses it at the ground next to me. "Millie," he says. In his eyes, I feel him telling me that everything is going to be okay. I feel him telling me I'll survive this. "Open it."

Lianna keeps her sword poised at him, but looks to me. She wonders if I'm up to something, but decides to play along. She says, "Do it."

"Heh," Gus says a laugh. He doesn't actually laugh. He just says it. "Yeah. *Do it*."

I drag the sack closer. It's smooth, leathery. The stitching is thick, rough. Haphazard at best. Looking closely at the black and white lines, I realize what they look like. Following them to the bottom of the bag, I see a spider. A black widow tattoo. "Oh God," I say.

"What's in the bag?" Lianna screams. She raises the sword, ready to swing down at me.

Oh God. Oh God. Oh God. I unknot the drawstring. God dammit. I tug the opening wider, and yeah. It's exactly the worst thing it could be. I still screech when I see Ellis's head glaring up at me. His lower lip quivering. I shove the bag away, screaming.

Lianna dives over the bag and lifts out her father's head. As she raises it, the bag falls inside out. It's all attached. His skin. His severed head. It's all still together, loosely stitched, hanging off his neck like a spent handkerchief. “Lianna screams. “What has he done to you?”

Ellis’s head blinks. His mouth motions God-knows what words to her.

“I normally do better work, but time was limited. Point is, the rest of ‘is body is somewhere on the east side o’ the building. Ya’ll think all yer li’l rats here can find his heart n’ put ‘im back together before dawn?”

Lianna puts a hand to Ellis’s cheek. A red tear trickles down his face. “Dad,” she whines. “My…” she trails off. She sets her father’s head down and picks up her sword. “Go!” she screams at the prairie dogs. “Find him! Find him!”

Prairie dogs pour from the roof. Some off the ledge. Others into vents. Gus claps his fists together. “Come on!” he growls. Lianna screams, raising her sword. The two monsters charge on either side of me. I’d like to say I use my instincts or cat like reflexes to leap safely out of the way. But I curl into a ball, cover my head, and scream as they collide. It’s not until Lianna’s sword swipes several hairs off my head that I stumble back, flail for traction, and back away in a frantic crab walk.

Gus, for such an enormous dump truck of a man, is quick on his feet. He dodges the blade over and over, chuckling as he dances around the vampire. “Come on!” He laughs. “Come on, bitch!”

Lianna isn’t having it. She thrusts the blade straight into Gus’s bulging gut. She screams, twisting the sword, pushing it deeper. Gus coughs blood onto her face. He looks down and watches the weapon go through him. Is that it? Is it over?

Not by a longshot. His left arm swings up in a wild haymaker, holding a .357 Magnum. He sets the barrel on the bridge of Lianna’s button nose, winks, and pulls the trigger. Lianna flies backwards, ripping the sword from Gus’s gut. They both hit the ground, motionless in a long, lingering silence.

“You bastard,” Lianna says, lifting her head. Strings of brain stretch from the exit wound. They twist, then grasp the back of her head. They swell, pulse, and seal the wound. Blood gushes out of her nostrils. She smirks.

Gus shoves entrails back into himself. He says, “So ya ready fer a fight or are ye ready fer a fight?”

Lianna picks up her sword. They stand. The charge again, Gus firing his gun and Lianna dodging bullets. They collide and–I don't even know how-Lianna throws Gus over her shoulder, smashing him through the rooftop access door. From the stairwell he yells, "Woo!" He dashes back into view. Lianna is already lunging at him, raising the sword over her head. They clash again, but I don't care. I've had enough. I'm done. I'm gone. I'm gone! The roof access door is gone and I am out of here.

Par for the course, I make it about seven steps without incident.

Gus's severed hand bounces off my head, to which I very elegantly yelp and flail my arms. The same sophisticated technique I'd use to brush surprise spiders out of my hair. It flops onto the ground and I continue to run into the stairwell. I take the first flight down so quick that I smack into the wall while trying to negotiate the turn. At the base of the second landing, I trip over my own foot, but keep moving. Two more flights down, I trip and again and this time crumble to my knees.

"Go," I command myself. "Go! Go!" I get back to my feet and pivot to make the turn. "No!" Several prairie dogs are on the next landing. They all look up at me. One of them barks. "Okay," I say. "Okay. I'm not here to hurt you. I just want to get by. That's all. That's all." I put up my hands as a friendly gesture. For all the good it'll do me. These are the same monsters that have been chasing me all night. Every time I look into their eyes they're picturing horrible and graphic things to do to me. In my defense, it's not like anybody's written an article on the subject. From the Discovery Channel I know what to do in the event of snake bites, bear attacks, skunk sprayings, and any number of worst case woodland scenarios. Having survived this long against them may as well make me the world's leading authority on the subject but I still have no idea what to do. They all hiss and scramble up the stairs at me. I turn. There's a door. I run through, yanking it shut.

I'm okay. I've made it. I take a few steps back. The sounds of barking and screeching is safely on the far side of the door. Several little claws appear at the bottom and shred the hallway carpet. The door thumps a few times. More claws stab through and drag back. They're digging. I turn again. I run. I don't even know where. I pass several hotel rooms and start turning door knobs in search of somewhere to hide. I scream for help. I keep moving, keep trying to find an escape. I pass a door and it opens. "What's going on?" a man says.

"Oh thank you!" I cry. "Thank you! Thank you!" I don't have time to explain. I don't even know how to explain. I step toward his door, toward sanctuary.

"Hang on! Are you all right? You're a mess? What happened?"

"Thank you," I say. "Please. You have to hide me."

Another door opens. "Will you be quiet?" An old woman hisses. "We're trying to sleep."

The man puts his hand up to stop me as I try to shove my way past him. "Hang on. Hang on! What are you doing?"

The old woman snaps, "Should I call the front desk?"

"Please," the man says.

The hallway vent breaks open just over his head. Several prairie dogs rain down, all of them clinging to his body and biting down. He screams. The woman across the hall screams. I scream. Several more prairie dogs leap from the woman's room, tackling her in a mist of blood. Down the hall a door bursts open and a naked man is writhing around, covered in prairie dogs. He smacks into the wall several times, gargles, and his head falls clean off. A woman appears from the room, covering herself with a sheet. "Leto!" she screams. "Leto!"

"Get out of here!" I scream, running again.

She doesn't stand a chance. Before I even finish my sentence, several prairie dogs are leaping off her companion, on to her. She falls back into room, trailed by a geyser of blood.

I round a corner, dashing down another hall. Then another. Where are the other stairwells in this place?

A crowd of maybe a dozen people are standing at an elevator, one of them pushing the button over and over. "Come on, come on!"

A little girl is crying. Her mother holds her. The father says, "It's okay, darling. There's just some rodents in the vents. We're going check out a little early."

"Go!" I charge at them. "Run! They're coming this way! Take the stairs!"

They look at me, but none of them move. The elevator dings and the doors open. The group starts pouring in, but there's a loud screech and the elevator car drops out of sight. The father shoves his daughter and wife away from the carnage. As I close in I see half of a person on the ground, his arm hanging down an empty elevator shaft. Prairie dogs are raining down. One lands on the carpet, stands on its hind legs, and hisses at the family. The mom kicks it back into the shaft, picking up her daughter in the same motion. "Go!" I scream. "Get out of here! Go!"

I keep running. It's all I can do. There's no safety. Only escape. Only far, far away from here. I have to keep moving. More doors open. More people are panicking, running for their lives. Some guy thrashes out of his room, accidentally elbowing me into the wall. Stars fill my eyes and I stumble to the ground. I suddenly become aware of just how much I'm sweating and how out of breath I am. My heart is pounding hard enough to break ribs. My ears are still ringing. But I can't slow down. Not now. Not after everything I've been dragged through tonight. I will make it to safety. I will make it home.

Several barks and squeaks catch my attention. I look into the nearest room, the one that guy side checked me away from. Most of a body flops off a bed as six prairie dogs lap blood from it.

Oh God. Keep moving.

My first few steps are slow, silent. As I continue to move I pick up speed. The thought occurs; this is just one floor. How far have the prairie dogs gotten? I've walked by this hotel plenty of times and there are at least fifteen stories. This place has hundreds of rooms and these prairie dogs are fighting their way into every last one of them.

Everyone here is going to die.

I stop running. I stop breathing.

I need to stop this. I need to do something. Anything.

There's a fire alarm down the hall. I pull it, wincing, expecting to be sprayed with ink or some chemical. The entire floor comes alive with flashing lights and blaring sirens. Water starts raining down everywhere. Throughout the halls I hear little barks and squeaks. An automated voice says, "There is an emergency. Please calmly proceed to the nearest exit.

There is an emergency. Please calmly proceed to the nearest exit."

I know it's stupid, but I'm somewhat disappointed that no ink or dye sprayed from the fire alarm.

Okay, I think. That'll help clear people out. Not everybody. I need to get rid of the prairie dogs. The fire alarm has a glass cabinet next to it with a hose, fire extinguisher, and oh- an ax. I try to pull the locker open, but there's no handle! Why is there no- Because I have to break the glass. I kick it in and pull the ax through. Okay, I think. Okay. When I killed Charles I turned back from ghoul to human. So if the vampire who made all of these prairie dogs dies, they'll all turn back to normal. I saw Lianna's memory of Ellis turning them, but now he's a severed head and more or less still going strong. I'd need to find his heart. So no luck there. But Lianna made Ellis. He's just a severed head right now, so if I kill her, he loses the vampirism. He dies. All the prairie dogs turn to normal.

I won't know how to find Ellis's heart without Gus and he's fighting Lianna. That's my only option. I have to kill Lianna.

I go for the stairs and the ceiling blows out down the hallway. Drywall gets everywhere. Gus falls through the hole with Lianna on top of him, stabbing him repeatedly with her sword. Gus grabs the sword by the handguard and pulls it closer. Lianna comes with it and he punches her across the jaw. They wrestle back and forth a moment, eventually smashing through the wall, into one of the rooms. "Okay," I say. "Okay. Just going to go murder a vampire." I raise the ax and start toward their fight.

As I move closer another wall blows out. Lianna is over Gus again, beating him down with his own arm. She screams, "How do you like it? How do you fucking like it?"

He laughs. Of course he laughs. He mule kicks her off him, sending her through another wall. He picks up his arm and looks my way. "Millie?" He says like he hasn't seen me in years. He reattaches his arm. Just as the wound starts to heal, Lianna's hands come up through the floor, grabs him by the ankles, and pulls him through.

"What am I doing?" I either think or say aloud. I inch my way to the hole in the floor. I have to do this. I have to kill her. Beneath the blaring alarms, panicked screams, and constant barking, I can hear Gus hooting. His laughter carries throughout the halls. I squat at the hole in the floor and toss the ax down. Slowly I lower myself, gripping onto the shredded carpet. I let go and drop the rest of the way. The next floor down is a mess. Some people are running through. Sprinklers are washing blood off the walls, but it's pooling into the carpet. I follow several large dents in the walls. A door is shattered so I follow it into the room just in time to see Gus and Lianna fall off a balcony together, Gus with several prairie dogs on him. Several other beasts follow. Several stay on the balcony, watching. I squeeze the ax. Okay, I think. I can't kill them, but if I hack them apart, they'll be slowed down enough to no longer be a threat. Then hopefully they won't be able to heal in the next few minutes. I'll clear a path to Lianna.

My approach is slow. Silent. Shaking and jittery, but silent. Four prairie dogs look off the balcony at something. They're distracted. I can do this. I tell myself over and over as I pass a dead body on the bed. It's some woman; her entire torso is a hollow cavity. I'm not so sure I can do this.

I take another step. Suddenly the woman's face explodes outward and a prairie dog, Spaz, is standing in her skull, barking at me with his paws pointed at my face. The other four prairie dogs dramatically look over their shoulders. Then they charge.

One swing. That's all I get. One swing and I think I at least made contact with one of them. But suddenly four prairie dogs are on top of me, all of them biting and digging their claws into my skin. I scream. I writhe, trying to shake them off. One bites into my knee I and tumble over the balcony.

I crush several prairie dogs when I land, but smack hard onto a tile floor. The balcony doesn't lead outside. I've landed next to an indoor swimming pool. For a second I see Gus and Lianna splashing around, trying to drown each other. But then a prairie dog leaps onto my chest and bites down. Followed by another. And another. They're bleeding me. Draining me. I try to kick but I can't feel like my legs. My arms are going numb. My head hurts. Everything hurts. It's getting dark.

That'll do pig.

No! I have to stop this. I lift my head as best I can. I try to shake the prairie dogs off, but only manage to nuzzle my face into one's side. So I bite it. I bite down, and it breaks easier than biting into melon. My mouth fills with blood. I swallow. I choke but more blood flows from the prairie dog so I continue to drink. I lift both arms, pressing it hard against my face. Its claws slice my cheeks but I just bite harder. I sit up. I stare down the other prairie dogs and they've all stopped their attack. They watch and almost casually hop off of me to sit and stare. One of them barks. Another grunts. I must be dizzy from the fall, because it sounds like they're actually speaking. I drink the prairie dog dry and drop it to the floor. It takes several steps but flops to its side, limp. Not dead. I can feel its heart. I look into its eyes and it wants me to feed it. The other prairie dogs sniff me, confused. One puts a paw on my foot and tilts its head. I look down at myself. All of my wounds are sealing. My uniform is shredded. My skin is somehow even more pasty than usual. I take a breath and- Yep. I have fangs.

A prairie dog barks, but it sounds like it's saying, "One of us!"

Other prairie dogs bark. "One of us!" They all say. Others join in. "One of us! One of us! One of us!"

"Millie?" Gus says from the pool. "What did you-"

Lianna leaps out of the water, tackling Gus from behind. They both go under. The floor shakes. An enormous bubble comes up the middle of the pool. It's draining. The prairie dogs watch as more and more of Gus and Lianna slugging each other becomes visible. A few vents and doors break open. More prairie dogs scamper into the room, many of them soaked in blood.

"Kill her!" I scream. "Gus! Kill her and the prairie dogs will turn back to normal!"

"What ya'll think I been tryin' ta do the past twenty minutes?" he screams back, head butting Lianna before punching her in the neck. Lianna grabs Gus by the shoulders and slams him against the side of the pool.

Okay. Okay. I have to help. I look around. Dozens of prairie dogs are filtering in around me. Some stop to sniff me. Others just walk on by. Many of them are barking to each other. They sounds like-wait, that doesn't even make sense.

Their barks sound like they're saying, "He's not here. The heart! It is not here!"

"What?" Lianna screams. She kicks Gus across the jaw so hard that it unhinges. "What do you mean he's not here?"

Gus chuckles, taking several more kicks to the gut. He resets his jaw and says, "Almost dawn."

I take a step forward and stub my toe against something. The ax is by my feet. Okay. Okay. I pick it up. It feels so light. Much lighter than it had a few minutes ago.

Lianna grabs Gus by the head and squeezes down with both hands, driving her thumbs into his eyeballs. "No," she screams. "No! No! No! No!"

I run forward, kicking prairie dogs aside with every step. Gus drops to the ground. He kicks Lianna up into the air and I raise the ax. I leap for it. It's all so effortless. I fly over the entire pool. Lianna hits the ceiling. She starts to fall. I fly forward-literally flying. I'm flying! I drive the ax into her back. We float over the prairie dogs, over the tile floor. Lianna smacks into the window, the ax stabbing right through her, digging into the glass. She hisses and flails, but I hold her steady. Over her shoulder, the first light of dawn glimpses over some distant buildings. My face starts to feel warm.

"Get behind me, girl!" Gus screams, shoving me aside. He presses Lianna's arms against the window. The vampire struggles but it's no use. Sunlight starts filling the pool room. All the prairie dogs' noses start to smoke.

Lianna screams, "This isn't over. I'll have your soul, ghoul! I'll have your soul!"

"Yeah. That's what yer daddy said. See that there small fire? The one a few rooftops over?"

"No!" Lianna pounds her face against the glass. She fights against Gus, but his grip is too strong. She screams, "Save me! My children! Father! Save me!"

The prairie dogs are barking frantically at each other. Most are turning and running. Many of them are saying, "Dayglow! Dayglow!" I spot the one I bit try to drag itself away. I take a step toward it, but as I step out of Gus's shadow, everything burns. I step back, watching as sunlight falls over the creature. It looks over its shoulder at me, ignites in a white flame, and then explodes. The tiles shatters around it. Several other prairie dogs are sent flying away. They combust in the air.

The floor shakes. Prairie dogs are popping everywhere.

"Hang on, girl!" Gus says.

Before I even know what to say, I'm yanked up the floor, into Gus's arms. I scream at the pain of the sunlight as he kicks Lianna's flaming body through the window, following her out into the morning air.

We drop. I scream bloody murder. Lianna burns beneath us like a meteor falling into the atmosphere. Windows in the hotel blow out as we pass. Floor after floor of vampire prairie dogs are exploding in the morning light. I feel one final blast of heat beneath us. Gus slams his feet into the pavement as whatever remains of Lianna bursts into cloud of red ash.

It takes a minute, or maybe several, but eventually I stop screaming. Gus lets go of me and I drop to the cement, trembling.

"Woo!" Gus says as the bones in his shins snap back into his body. "Woo! Didja see that?"

I'm a little too busy saying, "Oh my God! Oh my God! Oh my God!" to respond.

"I blown up vampires b'fore but never like that! And you! Li'l Missy, ye were great in there! Twice! Twice ya turned n' twice you turned back. Ain't nobody never done that before. Not even once."

Towering over us, the Hotel Renaissance is engulfed in flames. I start registering all the people around. Hundreds. The hotel staff. Guests. Police and firefighters are arriving on scene. "You bastard!" I scream at Gus, smacking him hard across the face. "You- You fucking bastard!"

"What? We got outta there," he shrugs.

"All those people! They all died because of you! I died because of you!"

Gus shrugs. He looks at me like I missed something.

"You told the vampires to come here! You picked the spot."

"Well, yeah. Highest part o' town at dawn. Earliest sunrise."

"Those people died! Don't you get that?"

"What? You don' think they'll get inta Heaven 'r somethin'?"

My right hook is nothing against his jaw, but I put every last part of myself into it.

"Millie? Damn!"

Some of the nearby officers trot over. One says, "Ma'am, you need to calm down!"

I punch Gus again. He puts up a hand. I think to strike me, so I flinch. But he looks at the cops. "She's jus' dealin' with some rough stuff, boys. Best just let 'er wear herself out."

"Wear myself out? Don't you care? You killed me!" I let another fist fly. He takes it.

The officers watch this a moment. All of their shoulders relax and they turn away. "Just blowing off some steam," one says. "It's fine."

I pick up the ax. Its blade is glowing gold from being lodged in Lianna. I raise it over my head. I'm about to send it into Gus's skull, but pause when I hear barking.

It's coming from the hotel. Standing in the lobby entrance are a group of twenty or so prairie dogs, out of the sun; surrounded by flames. The one in the middle has a white mohawk. Spaz. He barks. He's telling me, "You murdered my human. My Lianna. My horde." In his eyes I see Lianna lying in a desert, dying in the moonlight. The prairie dog bites its own paw and lets several drops fall.

Gus scratches his head. "Why didn't they turn back?"

Spaz barks again. "This isn't over." He turns and runs into the lobby, into the flames. As his minions turn to join him, I see my gruesome death in each of their eyes.

This is how I came to meet the Ultimate Hog Monster, Gus. This is why he stayed with me. But not why I stayed with him.

ACKNOWLEDGEMENTS

Thank you Taylor Young for all of your edits and putting up with Gus's dialogue.

Thanks to my beta readers; Tom Budday, Nathan Squires, Crissy Irwin, Courtney Drake, and Toni Bunton for all your commentary and support.

Thank you Natalie Schunk for your art of cover art and images of Millie and the vampires.

Thank you Crissy Irwin for your *about the author* image, Blue Donut Books logo, and all the wonderful book covers you've done for me.

And special thanks goes out to my parents, Jim and Joanne, and my brothers; Mike, Josh, Dan, and Chris. Corrine Camero, Lianna Trimble, Mike Bennett, Chris Morphy, Steve Pingilley, Ben Wilde, Josh Squires, Dan Jones, Caroline Maun, Michelle Foresman-Cooper, Annie Sorge, and Yoshi Bird.

Will… wherever you are, man. YOLO.

And of course, Guiness the prairie dog. One day we'll meet again on the rainbow bridge.

NECROMANTICA

The Kingdom of Fortia faces an apocalypse. Orcs have invaded from the East, massacring their way straight to the holy city Dromn. While the kingdom makes its final stand, a mysterious necromancer elf and her human companion plunge through the battle in a high stakes mission to loot the king's palace. But with the city aflame and the battle stretching to every horizon, can they pull of the greatest heist ever? Can they even escape with their lives?

WHISPER

In a standalone companion story to *Necromantica*, Lector Ara, a king thought to have died in a bear attack, awakens in his coffin, guided by a mysterious voice telling him that his kingdom and family are in danger.

TENDER BUTTONS TWO:
DISCO WRECKLORD

In 1914, American writer Gertrude Stein published the original Tender Buttons, a masterpiece in verbal cubism. Today, we live in a world of unnecessary reboots and sequels. So it shouldn't come as any surprise that we proudly present Tender Buttons Two: Disco Wrecklord, in which famed poet and muse Gertrude Stein has taken the English language hostage. It's up to the grammar police of Scotland Yard to diffuse, edit, and clarify her madness before she conjugates run on sentences improper loop loop slipping away, away, away There is no there there.

BONNIE BEFORE THE BRAIN IMPLANTS

EXPONENTIAL INNOVATIONS: BOOK ONE

Exponential Innovations' newest employee is Bonnie Neman; one of the greatest mind's the world will ever know, a recent college graduate, and therefore qualified only for an entry level position. As an introduction to this sci-fi comedy series, Bonnie tours several labs in new her workplace, repeatedly discovering just how easy it is to reach out and touch the impossible.

ABOUT THE AUTHOR

Keith Blenman hails from Metro Detroit where he teaches forensic analysis and works in a retail warehouse. He is short, chubby, and heavily tattooed.

OTHER BOOKS BY THIS AUTHOR

Please visit your favorite retailer to discover other books by Keith Blenman:

THE VECRIS

Whisper: A prelude to Necromantica
Necromantica
Ferrelf (coming soon)

ROADSIDE ATTRACTION

Book One: Siren Night
Book Two: Tramp Stamp Vamp
Book Three: Ruff Stuff (coming soon-ish)

OTHER FICTION

Bartered Breath
Black Friday
Bonnie Before The Brain Implants
Braaaaaains
Entrees & Statistics
Tender Buttons Two: Disco Wrecklord
Where Dogs Sweat

NON-FICTION

Character Development for Badass Writers

Millie and Gus will return in

ROADSIDE ATTRACTION

PART THREE

RUFF STUFF

CONNECT WITH KEITH BLENMAN

I hope you enjoyed my book. I love to connect with fans, readers, and critics alike, so please check out my social media sites. Reviews on Goodreads, Amazon, iTunes, and other retailers are also always appreciated.

Twitter: **@keithblenman**

Instagram: **@blenmankeith**

Facebook.
http://www.facebook.com/keithblenmanwriter/

Subscribe to Keith's blog:
http://keithblenman.blogspot.com

FOR MORE ART BY NATALIE SCHUNK

Instagram: **@Natalie.Schunk**

Tumbler:
http://natalie-schunk.tumblr.com/

FOR MORE ART BY CHRISTINA IRWIN

Instagram: **@Lady_Mustela**

Portfolio:
http://crissyirwin1983.wixsite.com/portfolio

Get Christina's art on t-shirts:
https://floopthe ferret.threadless.com/

www.ingramcontent.com/pod-product-compliance
Lightning Source LLC
Chambersburg PA
CBHW060611310726
48982CB00003B/518